P9-CRS-308

That was why she'd returned to Serendipity. To find this man.

Rebecca stared silently into the cowboy's sad yet angry blue eyes.

He was definitely flummoxed by her question.

"Who *am* I?" Tanner repeated her question incredulously. "Rebecca, what are you talking about?"

"I feel like I should recognize you," she admitted, feeling the heat rising to her cheeks. "No. I *know* I should. But I…I'm sorry. My mind isn't cooperating. I'd hoped— Well, if anything would give my memory the jolt it needed to return, this would have been it. And yet I don't know who you are, other than your name. Tanner Hamilton?"

His expression clouded with confusion.

"Of course, I'm—" He paused. "Wait. Are you trying to say you really don't know your own husband?" He removed his hat by the crown and threaded his fingers through his thick blond hair.

He needed a haircut, Rebecca thought, but then realized what an odd observation that was for her to make. It was somehow…*personal.*

A *Publishers Weekly* bestselling and award-winning author with over 1.5 million books in print, **Deb Kastner** writes stories of faith, family and community in a small-town Western setting. She lives in Colorado with her husband and a pack of miscreant mutts, and is blessed with three daughters and two grandchildren. She enjoys spoiling her grandkids, movies, music (The Texas Tenors!), singing in the church choir and exploring Colorado on horseback.

Books by Deb Kastner

Love Inspired

Cowboy Country

Yuletide Baby
The Cowboy's Forever Family
The Cowboy's Surprise Baby
The Cowboy's Twins
Mistletoe Daddy
The Cowboy's Baby Blessing
And Cowboy Makes Three
A Christmas Baby for the Cowboy
Her Forgotten Cowboy

Christmas Twins

Texas Christmas Twins

Email Order Brides

Phoebe's Groom
The Doctor's Secret Son
The Nanny's Twin Blessings
Meeting Mr. Right

Visit the Author Profile page at Harlequin.com for more titles.

Her Forgotten Cowboy

Deb Kastner

PAPL
DISCARDED

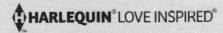

If you purchased this book without a cover you should be aware
that this book is stolen property. It was reported as "unsold and
destroyed" to the publisher, and neither the author nor the
publisher has received any payment for this "stripped book."

Recycling programs
for this product may
not exist in your area.

LOVE INSPIRED BOOKS

ISBN-13: 978-1-335-47938-9

Her Forgotten Cowboy

Copyright © 2019 by Debra Kastner

All rights reserved. Except for use in any review, the reproduction
or utilization of this work in whole or in part in any form by any
electronic, mechanical or other means, now known or hereafter
invented, including xerography, photocopying and recording, or in
any information storage or retrieval system, is forbidden without
the written permission of the editorial office, Love Inspired Books,
195 Broadway, New York, NY 10007 U.S.A.

This is a work of fiction. Names, characters, places and incidents are
either the product of the author's imagination or are used fictitiously, and
any resemblance to actual persons, living or dead, business establishments,
events or locales is entirely coincidental.

This edition published by arrangement with Love Inspired Books.

® and TM are trademarks of Love Inspired Books, used under license.
Trademarks indicated with ® are registered in the United States Patent
and Trademark Office, the Canadian Intellectual Property Office and in
other countries.

www.Harlequin.com

Printed in U.S.A.

If we believe not,
yet he abideth faithful: he cannot deny himself.
—*2 Timothy* 2:13

To my husband, Joe.
I almost lost you to a double stroke.
I praise God every day that He's given us
a second chance.
You are my love and my best friend forever.

Chapter One

Everybody knew.

Tanner Hamilton stood stiff-spined, arms crossed and his knees locked tight, front and center on the makeshift auction block located on the community green at Serendipity, Texas's First Annual Bachelors and Baskets Auction, and scanned the entirely too enthusiastic audience. Sweat beaded his brow and made his black T-shirt stick to his skin.

It was ripping him up inside to be standing out here at the center of a public venue with everyone's eyes upon him. If they weren't judging him, then at the very least he spotted pity in some of their eyes. It was a small town. His friends and neighbors— everyone in his acquaintance and probably some who weren't, had heard about poor Tanner Hamilton.

It wasn't like he was the only man in the world whose wife had ever left him, but he might as well have been, for the way he was feeling.

His heart was in shreds and there was nothing he could do to hide it.

He clenched his fists against his biceps as he forced a breath into his burning lungs. Tension rolled off his shoulders, leaving his neck stiff and unmovable.

He hated when people stared at him. This whole experience made him feel more like he was on a chopping block than the auction block. He wasn't much in the mood for community events these days, especially because he was pretty sure he could guess what was going through the crowd's minds right about now.

Poor Tanner. His wife went and left him without a word about where she's gone. Why'd she do it? It is always hard to tell in cases like these. It could be she was at fault. Then again, maybe Tanner had somehow run her off.

Run her off?

No.

He gritted his teeth even harder to keep from shouting that one single, defensive word out loud.

No.

He might be guilty of a thousand things in his relationship with his wife—*many* thousands of things, if he were being honest—but not that. He hadn't told her to leave.

He hadn't told her anything.

Most of these folks from around here knew who the true injured party in his relationship with his wife was—and it wasn't him. Maybe it was his pride talkin'. Maybe not. He'd had plenty of time to mull over what had gone on between them during the rough times, and even though he knew they had more than their fair share of problems and trials for a young couple, he still couldn't imagine what could have suddenly set Rebecca off to the point where she would purposefully choose to ignore the wedding vows she'd made to him to love him for better or for worse.

Where were those vows now?

He couldn't say. He didn't even know where *she* was.

He would admit, but only to himself, that maybe what they'd been facing at the time had been *worse* for both of them, especially Rebecca, but *he* wouldn't have run away from their problems, no matter what. When he'd said, *To have and to hold, from this day forward until death do us part*, he'd meant every single solitary word.

Rebecca, on the other hand? Not so much.

So they'd drifted apart in those last few months before she'd left him. That happened at some point in every marriage, right? It wasn't all roses and sunshine all the time.

He was a simple rancher with an equally simple philosophy about how to love his God and live his life. A man dealt with whatever circumstances God gave him without complaining. Sometimes it was good, sometimes not so much. Some things a man could plan for, see the storms coming so he could batten down the hatches. Other times things came unexpectedly, or didn't come at all. Sometimes life swung a fisted punch in a gut which was hard to recover from, and no doubt about it. But a real man had to pick himself up, dust himself off and keep on keeping on. That's how he ran his ranch, and up until a short while ago, that's how he'd *believed* he'd kept his marriage alive and stable.

Maybe not, though. If he'd paid more attention, maybe—

But a dozen *maybes* wouldn't bring Rebecca back to him.

Even with all the problems between them, most especially the heartbreaking pain of them suffering through the seven months' stillbirth of their firstborn daughter, whom they'd named Faith before they buried her in the ground, he never would have imagined Rebecca would out-and-out abandon him.

But six months ago, she had.

After they'd buried their daughter, Rebecca had spent weeks in bed, not even allowing him to open the curtains to let some sunshine in or turn on the lights. She didn't want to have anything to do with her life anymore—or with him. He'd taken to sleeping on the couch so as not to disturb her. She took pills for anxiety and insomnia, but they didn't really help her.

And then he'd come back in late from his ranch work one evening and she'd been gone. No note or anything. No explanation.

Just *gone*.

She'd disappeared to no-one-knew-where, not even her mother, and she'd only called him once since the day she'd walked out on him.

She had been reaching out to him with that one phone call, and in hindsight, he realized he should have taken the time to listen to her, to try to talk through their problems and bring her back home. But she'd caught him off guard on an evening when he was already feeling down. And when he'd picked up the telephone and heard her voice, he'd been so angry he hadn't even let her speak. He'd understood why they called it seeing red, because that's exactly how it felt.

And to his shame, he hadn't let her say a word. He just hung up on her.

He didn't know whether to be glad or sad or mad that she'd taken the hint and hadn't attempted to reach out to him again.

Probably a mixture of all three.

In any case, he didn't belong up here on a bachelor's auction block. He was a man unhappily separated from his wife and he didn't want anything to do with women. Full stop. It didn't matter to him that every man in Serendipity, married and single alike, was offering his services for this very special auction.

Tanner just wanted to go home. Alone. To grieve in private.

If he hadn't promised Jo Spencer, the boisterous old redhead who was both organizer and auctioneer, that he'd do his part for charity, a fund-raiser to build a local senior center recently approved by the town council, Tanner wouldn't be here at all. He would have stayed home at his ranch where he belonged. At least out on the range with his horse and the cattle he could nurse his broken heart in peace and quiet.

Well, not exactly *peace*, anymore. Nor quiet, for that matter.

He no longer had that luxury.

"Uncle Tanner! Uncle Tanner!"

He looked down to the front row of the crowd to see his three-year-old niece, Mackenzie, madly giggling, bouncing up and down and waving at him, as excited about this outing as Tanner was not. Tanner's mother-in-law, Peggy, Rebecca's mom, was attempting without much success to corral the small girl, whose blond curls bobbed right along with the rest of her body. She had more energy in her pinky finger than Tanner had in his whole body on a good day. She also had the biggest blue eyes Tanner had ever seen—and she knew just how to use them to melt his heart.

But it wasn't her fault none of the adults around her could get their lives together.

Mackenzie deserved his very best, so he made a gigantic effort to smile and wave back at her. Hopefully it looked like a smile and not a grimace, for the child's sake.

Five months ago, Tanner's sister, Lydia, had landed in jail for the second time on drug charges, leaving her daughter, Mackenzie, temporarily in Tanner's care, as he was the only other living relative. Two major life changes in six months was two too many, but Tanner was determined to do whatever it took to protect and provide for Mackenzie. He was incredibly grateful for Peggy, who had cheerfully moved to the ranch to help with the round-the-clock care the preschooler demanded.

Peggy had never questioned Tanner's loyalty to Rebecca, even though their relationship had come to such an abrupt ending. In Peggy's mind—and in Tanner's— she was still family, and always would be.

Mackenzie's arrival in Tanner's life was the ultimate irony. Rebecca had left him because the stress of losing their daughter was more than Rebecca had been able to handle, and she'd become withdrawn and moody, which Tanner frankly couldn't comprehend.

For whatever reason, or maybe many reasons, she'd eventually left him altogether.

And then only a few months later, Mackenzie had entered his life.

If Rebecca had stayed, maybe she could have healed her heart by caring for the precious little girl God had brought into Tanner's life. They would have been a family.

Rebecca's most heartfelt wish was to be a mother, and she would have been such a good mother figure for Mackenzie. She'd had so much love to give a child.

If only she were here to take on that role now. What a difference that would have made.

But she wasn't here, leaving Tanner a single man trying his best to juggle ranch life with finding quality time with Mackenzie.

"Go, Uncle Tanner!" Mackenzie called, joyfully clapping her little hands. "Yay for Uncle Tanner!"

Tanner breathed out heavily and flashed a puppy-dog glance at Jo, hoping she might take pity on him and release him from this painful obligation, but she just smiled encouragingly and opened the bidding.

"As y'all know, Tanner here is a lifelong rancher. Need your fences repaired or your tack buffed to a shine? Tanner's your man. Need help rounding up stray calves? You're looking at the answer to your problem right here with this handsome fella."

To Tanner's surprise, within moments, folks were cheerfully tossing out bids, merrily one-upping each other to win what Tanner considered not a particularly great prize.

He should have expected this, he belatedly realized. His friends and neighbors were eager to support him throughout these tough months and this was one concrete way they could do it, showing him a little love by their high bids. Of course they felt sorry for him and Mackenzie, but it wasn't the kind of pity that put a man down. They were trying to build him up.

He released his breath and tried to relax. This would be over in a minute. He'd worked himself into a dither for no reason. It wasn't his fault Rebecca had left him, and everyone in town knew it. He had a new appreciation for those willing to step up for him.

He would mend fences or round up cattle for the woman who won him to the best of his ability, and then his obligation to Serendipity's new senior center would be met.

He removed his dark brown Stetson and combed his fingers through his thick blond hair. He was overdue for a haircut. Rebecca had always trimmed it for him.

He nodded gratefully toward Bob and Janice Jones, an elderly couple near the back of the crowd who were currently the high bidders. Janice was a spunky ol' gal and blew him a kiss, which he captured with his hand and pressed to his cheek. He grinned, his first genuine smile of the day.

Sweet old lady.

Nearby, a young woman flicked her auburn hair off her forehead with her thumb and forefinger, and then shook it out again, causing her hair to drop right back into place over her copper-penny eyes, basically undoing what she'd just accomplished.

The air around him froze, lodging firmly in Tanner's throat. He tried to take a breath but choked on it. Coughing didn't help. His blood turned to lead in his veins and an iron fist gripped his heart, squeezing painfully.

Rebecca.

There was no question about it.

Her hair was longer now, closer to shoulder length than chin length, as it had been the last time he'd seen her, but he knew that nervous gesture as well as he knew the beat of his own heart. He'd seen it a million times before. Whenever something was bothering her or she was deep in thought, her hand went straight to her hair.

He'd once thought it was cute the way her bangs always swept right back down to brush her high cheekbones just after she'd pushed them aside. Now the gesture only made his gut churn until he thought he might be physically sick.

Janice Jones was still waving cash in the air and staying ahead of the other bidders, but Tanner couldn't wait for his lot to be finished. He didn't have a moment to spare if he was going to catch up to his wife.

Even now, Rebecca had picked up her backpack and was turning away, then walking toward the far edge of the park where a few townsfolk were already picnicking. He immediately noticed her limp. One of her legs was encased in a walking boot.

When had she been hurt? How?

If he didn't catch her now...

He shrugged an apology to Bob and Janice and bolted off the front of the platform, not even bothering to use the stairs. It was a six-foot drop to the ground and he landed hard, hitting it at a dead run.

"Pardon me. Excuse me. I'm sorry," he muttered as he threaded his way through the gathering, ignoring the buzz of surprise he'd created by his unexpected exit. He didn't care if he was creating drama the folks in town would gossip about for weeks.

The only thing on his mind was catching his wife.

"Rebecca," he called as he narrowed the distance between them. "Rebecca. Please. Wait!"

She neither turned nor paused. It was almost as if she didn't hear him.

Or else she was ignoring him, which was probably the more likely explanation. She was walking away from him again, just like the first time. But if that was the case, then...

Why was she here?

"Rebecca," he called again, just before he reached her side. His lungs burned from the effort of running. Working on a ranch, he was in good shape, but a runner he was not.

"Rebecca," he pleaded. "Hold up a minute."

He grabbed hold of her elbow and turned her around, only then realizing that in addition to her leg, her wrist was in a splint. Something bad had definitely happened.

Was that what she'd called him about that day? That she'd been hurt and needed his help?

And where had he been? Out on the range, nursing his own internal wounds.

Shame mixed with anger and warred deep within his chest.

But then again, he reminded himself, pressing his emotions back, none of this would have happened had she not left him in the first place.

"What's the deal?" he demanded, his raspy voice coming in short, unsteady breaths, half because of the dash he'd made to catch up with her and half because of nerves. It had never occurred to him that she might return today of all days.

Her eyes went wide with surprise, shock and concern. She glanced down at his hold on her elbow and took a physical step backward.

"Rebecca?" Frustration pulsed through him as she jerked out of his reach and tucked her good hand underneath the one in the splint. Why was she acting as if he were about to accost her?

"I—I'm sorry, I—" Rebecca stammered. She sounded lost. Confused. Maybe even a little frightened.

Of him?

Their marriage had not ended well, but he had never, *ever* given her a reason to fear him. He'd barely even raised his voice when they had arguments, which were few and far between, anyway.

Sure, they sniped at each other when they were tired, just like every other married couple in the world, but they hadn't fought much. That wasn't their way. Instead, resentment burned under the surface of their relationship but never emerged, so they'd drifted apart. Their rainbows-and-unicorns promise to each other that they would never let the sun go down on their anger just sort of slipped away into the twilight.

Yet despite everything that had happened, and even with what felt like an uncrossable rift between them, he had still loved her with his whole heart—

Until she'd betrayed him.

She had left him, not the other way around. She was the one who needed to make the first move. To reach out. To apologize.

Their eyes met and locked and he narrowed his gaze on her. There was something peculiar in the way she was looking at him, all glassy-eyed, her pupils dilated. It was almost as if she were looking through him rather than at him, as if she didn't recognize him.

"I am R-Rebecca." She sounded as if she wasn't entirely certain that was true. As if she didn't know her own name. Her dark red eyebrows lowered, shading her gaze. "But who are you?"

"What?" he asked, his voice rising in tone and pitch. He was thoroughly flummoxed by her question. She may as well just have physically pushed him. Her words had the same effect.

She took yet another step back and raised a protective hand, laying it across her burgeoning midsection.

For the first time since she'd turned around to face him, Tanner's gaze dropped to her stomach. His breath left his lungs as if he'd been sucker punched.

For a moment, his sight clouded, darkness tunneling his vision as the reality of his world tilted on its axis.

Rebecca was pregnant.

She knew her first name was Rebecca.

Rebecca Foster was the name she'd been born with and the one she remembered—even if her driver's license said something else.

She opened her hand and read the words written in black ink on her palm.

Check notes—cell phone.

Filled with both curiosity and anxiety, she glanced at her phone.

Hamilton.

Her name was Rebecca Hamilton.

She closed her eyes for a moment and repeated the name in her mind.

Hamilton. Hamilton.

Rebecca Hamilton.

There was something vaguely familiar about the sound of the name, and the butterflies currently flittering about in her tummy had nothing to do with her growing baby, but that was as far as it went.

She couldn't *claim* that name as hers. Nothing in her Swiss-cheese memory gave her that assurance.

According to the notes her best childhood friend, Dawn, had written to help her navigate her way in Serendipity, Rebecca was separated from her husband, Tanner.

Tanner.

Tanner Hamilton.

Her *husband*.

According to her notes, separated but not divorced.

She didn't believe in divorce—and she strongly felt that moral principle, the same way she still believed in God. Why she knew this when she couldn't put names to the faces of those she supposedly knew best confused her even more.

It made no sense to her that she could know some things absolutely and know absolutely nothing about others.

If she didn't believe in divorce, then why had she left this man—Tanner Hamilton?

She let that name roll around in her head for a moment, but again—nothing. It didn't matter how hard she tried, her memories would just not come. And trying harder, straining her already overloaded brain to retrieve them, only gave her a migraine.

Rebecca was sure Dawn had explained to her at some point *why* she was no longer in a relationship with Tanner, but she hadn't put an explanation in the notes on the phone and Rebecca couldn't recall a reason. Nor could she remember why Dawn had refused to come with her back to her hometown. She only knew that where Serendipity and Tanner were concerned, she was here on her own.

Everything had been so vague since the accident, but she knew Dawn had been a good friend to her, so she couldn't dismiss the nagging notion that her best friend did not like her husband, which she remembered from this morning when they'd had a heated discussion over why Rebecca should not return to Serendipity.

Dawn had reminded her that it was she who had stayed by her side the whole time, both in the hospital and afterward, caring for her and doing her best to supply the information Rebecca's mind refused to provide. At this point, what else could she do but trust that Dawn was telling her the truth?

That, and the fact that she remembered who Dawn was from high school. It was only the recent years that were a complete blank to her.

But while her memories were MIA, her emotions were present and accounted for, almost more than she could handle. Part of her wished she'd never come back, and part of her wanted to run away again even now. She'd never felt more anxious and awkward in her entire life—or at least the part of her life she remembered.

After the hit and run, Rebecca had been in the hospital for two weeks, suffering from a blow to the head, two cracked ribs, a bruised wrist and a broken ankle. Her ankle had required reconstructive surgery which had included metal plates and pins. Dawn had been riding in the passenger seat in the car with her but, thank the good Lord, had only suffered from minor cuts and bruises.

The doctor had told Rebecca it would be a while before she completely recuperated physically. Even a month after the incident, Rebecca still felt achy and sore and had a hard time sleeping. Muscles ached where she didn't even know she had muscles.

Ha. Amnesia joke. Her lips twitched despite her anxiety.

The biggest, most problematic injury had been her

memory, which was now spotty at best and sometimes left her at a complete blank. She remembered how to read but the next day she wouldn't be able to summarize what it was she'd read. She knew how to drive a car and had a handle on the rules of the road, but if she didn't have her notes with her and the GPS from her cell phone she'd forget where she was going. And she didn't even want to think about attempting to cook anything, even though she had a gut feeling she used to be someone who'd enjoyed spending time preparing meals. But now, if she wasn't careful, she was liable to burn the whole house down when she forgot she'd put something in the oven to roast.

But the most frustrating thing of all was she had no memory of the past few years. Relationships. People. Nada.

At least her faith in God hadn't left her, or she didn't know how she would be able to deal with everything she was now facing. She'd been six months' pregnant when the truck came out of nowhere and T-boned her sedan, and it was only an act of God that her baby was still safely cocooned in her womb.

No. Not *her* baby—

Their baby. The man standing in front of her was the baby's father.

It frightened her to look into Tanner's eyes and draw a complete blank. She had no memory of the man to whom she had once committed her heart and life. The man to whom she'd made sacred vows, and then, to her mortification and shame, had apparently found reason to break them.

That's why she'd returned to Serendipity. To find this man, to connect with her past, in the hope that seeing her husband again would trigger her thoughts and memories to return.

She stared silently into the cowboy's sad yet angry blue eyes, willing her memory to supply the information needed to appropriately place this tall, muscular man into the framework of her life.

He was definitely flummoxed by her question.

"Who *am* I?" He repeated her question incredulously. "Rebecca, what are you talking about?"

"I feel like I should recognize you," she admitted, feeling the heat rising to her cheeks. "No. I *know* I should. But I—I'm sorry. My mind isn't cooperating. I'd hoped—well, if anything would give my memory the jolt it needed to return, this would have been it. And yet I don't know who you are, other than your name. Tanner Hamilton?"

His expression clouded with confusion.

"Of course, I'm—" He paused. "Wait. Are you trying to say you really don't know your own husband?" He removed his hat by the crown and threaded his fingers through his thick blond hair.

He needed a haircut, Rebecca thought, but then realized what an odd observation that was for her to make. It was somehow...*personal*.

"Rebecca!" An older woman with her white hair pulled up high in a casual bun brushed past Tanner and tightly embraced Rebecca, tears flowing unheeded down her cheeks. A little blonde girl Rebecca guessed to be about three, who had been tightly grasping the woman's hand, now skittered behind Tanner, clutching his leg and peeking out from behind his knee, clearly startled by the woman's outburst.

"Honey, you're home." The older woman kissed Rebecca's cheek and cupped her face in her hands. "Oh, Rebecca. I was so worried. What happened to you?"

Rebecca's emotions resonated without prompting to this woman's embrace. It was a childlike, natural response to the woman whom she knew without a doubt.

When Rebecca closed her eyes, she pictured a much younger version of this woman, without the lines of stress that now creased her forehead and eyes. In the picture in Rebecca's head, her mother had the same bright auburn hair as Rebecca now possessed. She was making dinner in an old country kitchen, laughing and dancing with a handsome black-haired, blue-eyed man.

"Mama," she whispered, and her heart concurred.

"You're pregnant," her mother exclaimed, immediately pressing a hand to Rebecca's belly. "Oh, darling. The Lord blessed you and Tanner. I knew He wouldn't let you two down."

Tears pricked Rebecca's eyes and she nodded. She didn't miss the glance her mother flashed Tanner—one filled with something akin to fear.

But why would that be? Did her mother not consider this happy news because Rebecca and Tanner were at odds with one another?

A moment later, her mother's gaze turned back to her and filled with such joy that Rebecca decided maybe she'd mistaken or misread what she thought she'd seen a moment before. Her mother looked radiant as she whispered to Rebecca's womb, and Rebecca couldn't help the soft smile that escaped her as she laid her hand over her mother's and felt the baby kick.

Tanner didn't appear to share the same enthusiasm. His brow lowered and his jaw ticked with strain.

"The baby is moving well?" he asked.

Rebecca wasn't quite sure what he was asking, but apparently her mother did.

"Baby is kicking up a storm," her mother assured Tanner.

"I see." He ran a hand across his whiskered jaw. "So when were you planning to tell me you were pregnant with our child?" His voice was husky and still held an edge to it which Rebecca couldn't decipher. "Or were you just going to leave me in the dark?"

He was clearly unhappy with the news of the pregnancy. Did he not want a baby, other than the child clinging to his leg who was yet another stranger to Rebecca?

Was that why she'd left him? Because she'd wanted a family and he didn't? But somehow, that didn't seem right, either.

It was just so *weird*. Tanner was her recently estranged spouse and the father of her baby. And yet his face was that of a stranger. She felt no intimacy there.

It was too much for Rebecca to take in all at once and her emotions were going haywire.

And what about the little girl peeking out from behind his leg?

Who was she?

Their daughter?

There was no spark of recognition in Rebecca's heart regarding this little girl. She wasn't experiencing any kind of gut instinct suggesting she'd ever even seen the sweet preschooler before today, although that was a definite possibility, since the child appeared to be very comfortable not only with Tanner, but with Rebecca's mother, as well.

But the child wasn't hers. Surely she would remember *that*.

She might not remember who she was. She might have left Serendipity—and Tanner—for reasons she couldn't now fathom, but she would *never* abandon her own child.

She didn't need total recall to tell her that.

She crouched down to the girl's level and smiled.

"My name is Rebecca," she said softly. If only she knew more, if there were more for her to say. She wished the little girl didn't immediately draw away from her as if she were a stranger. For some reason, that hurt her heart.

"This is Mackenzie," Tanner said warily. "She's my sister Lydia's child. Your niece. You were with me at her christening, but I guess she's grown up a lot since then, so you probably wouldn't recognize her."

Rebecca stood and slanted Tanner a look. Was he mocking her, or giving her a way out of an uncomfortable situation? It was the not knowing that made her heart feel as if it were being squeezed by a fist.

"I think we'd better find someplace quiet to talk," her mother suggested. She threaded her arm through

Rebecca's, as if to reassure herself Rebecca was real and that she wouldn't be running away again.

That physical link reassured Rebecca, as well. She was not as all alone in the world as she currently felt.

Tanner gestured toward the community green, where many of the townsfolk had already spread out picnic blankets and were happily lunching together. It was becoming more crowded by the moment as the auction started to wind down.

"We aren't going to get any privacy here," he said. "This isn't the kind of conversation I want my neighbors to overhear."

"You're right. Besides, none of us has a picnic basket, anyway," Peggy pointed out. "I hadn't planned to bid on anyone today. Shall we go back to the ranch where we can talk in private?"

"The ranch?" Rebecca echoed.

We live on a ranch? Like with cows?

Dawn had told Rebecca she was a schoolteacher. Middle school math, although she was trained to teach anything from middle school through college. She remembered numbers and equations, and that had sounded good and right to her. It was instinctual. Numbers were solid. They didn't change.

But a ranch?

Talk about feeling way, *way* out of her comfort zone. She couldn't believe she would actually choose to marry a cowboy.

"Rebecca, did you drive here?" her mother asked, concern flashing across her gaze. And it was no wonder.

An amnesiac driving a car was a frightening thought, indeed.

Rebecca shook her head. "I used a car service."

"Super. Then you can ride back to the ranch with me. I'm living out there with Tanner now to help take care of the little one," she said by way of explanation. "And soon now it will be two little ones. How exciting."

Tanner's gaze met Rebecca's for a moment, and she doubted *exciting* would be a word either one of them would use right now. But her mother didn't appear to notice and continued speaking.

"Tanner, you take Mackenzie with you in your truck and we'll meet you back at the ranch."

Back at the ranch.

A place she didn't remember, but which she had evidently once called home.

Chapter Two

How could God do this to them?

Tanner gripped the steering wheel so tightly his knuckles turned white. He was trying to control his breathing so he didn't scare Mackenzie, but it wasn't easy to do. The air was coming in gasps and burning his lungs.

How could God let this happen to one family? It was almost more than he could bear.

He felt as if he were on some kind of nightmarish merry-go-round and he didn't know how to get off. He'd been half expecting to be served with legal documents soon, since his communication with Rebecca had been completely cut off—which he now regretted and for which he privately admitted at least partial responsibility. If he hadn't hung up when she'd reached out to him...

Instead of acting like a rational, mature adult, he'd let his anger, ego and pride get the best of him.

And now this.

Now he knew why she hadn't returned his phone

calls and texts. She'd been in the hospital recovering from a horrible car crash.

She—and their baby. He still wasn't certain what to do with the knowledge that they were expecting a child.

At the moment, all he could do was feel perplexed.

And amazed.

No matter what their past, it gutted him that Rebecca had been injured, could even have been killed. Thank God He'd taken care of them and things hadn't been worse than they were now.

Rebecca still suffering from the many physical injuries she'd sustained—and their unborn child somehow still safe in her womb.

Oh, dear Lord. Their *baby*.

And Rebecca's apparent amnesia—

What was he supposed to do about *that*? It was all so surreal. He didn't think things like that happened in real life. That was the stuff of television detective shows.

He pulled his truck up next to the ranch house and let Mackenzie out of her car seat in the back of the dual cab. He couldn't help but smile when she wrapped her trusting little arms around his neck so he could help her out of the vehicle.

The moment her little feet hit the ground, she squealed and went straight toward the herd of goats, her favorite ranch animal in all the world, she'd told him on multiple occasions. She held her hands out wide as if to hug the nearest goat. She giggled hysterically when one of the larger goats grabbed ahold of the hem of her shirt in its mouth and tugged.

The silly goats got into everything and drove Tanner crazy, but at least they kept the grass around the house under control.

It had been Rebecca's idea to get the herd in the first place. Like Mackenzie, Rebecca also loved those mischievous animals and often saved the dinner scraps for them—or at least, she'd used to, before she'd left him.

Before the accident that took her memory away.

Minutes later, Peggy arrived with Rebecca. For the longest time, the three of them stood in front of the house without speaking, watching Mackenzie play with the herd of goats.

Rebecca looked around wide-eyed, her expression filled with almost childlike wonder as she took in the scene—Mackenzie playing with the goats, and the chickens clucking in their coop, reminding Tanner that they hadn't yet gotten their midday meal. Tanner's small herd of horses milled about in a nearby pasture, and another small pasture on the other side of the ranch house contained Rebecca's most beloved small herd of alpacas.

After visiting a wool festival and getting to meet live alpacas, she had gotten this crazy idea into her head that she wanted alpacas of her own. She'd done her research and then presented her idea to Tanner. He'd never been able to deny her anything, so before he knew it, they were proud owners of a half-dozen alpacas, which she'd carefully grown in numbers. Rebecca would gather their wool and spin it, often spending her evenings knitting by the fire in the winter and out on the front porch in the spring and on mild summer nights.

He watched her expression when her gaze landed on the alpacas, feeling as if his heart stopped beating as he waited and hoped for even the smallest sign of recognition. But to his surprise, her face tightened with strain. Her lips pressed together tightly and her brow furrowed over her nose. She brushed her hair back, only to have the locks fall forward again a moment later.

Peggy's gaze met Tanner's and she gave him a brief nod. She'd noticed Rebecca's odd reaction, too.

"Let's go inside and get comfortable, and then we can chat," Peggy suggested airily, as if they had invited a good friend over—a guest, and not her daughter and his wife. "Rebecca, do you prefer coffee or tea?"

Coffee, Tanner thought. He used to tease her that she liked a little coffee with her cream and sugar.

Rebecca's gaze shifted to Tanner and then back to Peggy.

"I—I don't know."

"Coffee it is, then," Tanner said, jumping in to relieve Rebecca's discomfiture. "Don't worry. I know just how you like it."

Rebecca nodded, her copper eyes turning glassy with tears.

Tanner's chest tightened. What had he said that would make her start crying? They were talking about coffee, not their breakup. Her tears had always had a way of punching him right in the gut, and despite the time and distance that had been between them, that much hadn't changed.

He was only trying to help, but he'd somehow made things worse.

Over coffee.

Peggy and Rebecca settled in the living room and

Mackenzie dug into her toy box in the corner. She'd quickly warmed up to Rebecca and was now showing Auntie Rebecca this and that, chattering about her favorite toys while Tanner made coffee in the kitchen.

Rebecca dutifully exclaimed in delight as Mackenzie exhibited her very favorite doll.

The tension, which seemed to have eased somewhat when Tanner was watching from the kitchen, immediately rematerialized the moment Tanner entered the room.

"Here," he said, offering a mug to Rebecca. "Taste it and see what you think."

Rebecca sipped at the coffee, which was a light mocha color due to all the cream and sugar Tanner had dumped into it. Her expression relaxed.

"This is really good. Thank you."

Tanner let out a breath he hadn't even realized he'd been holding. Everything else in their lives had changed, and he hadn't been positive that wouldn't have included Rebecca's taste in coffee, as well.

Did amnesia even work that way?

He really was clueless, and didn't have the slightest idea where to start.

He looked around, wondering where to sit. Rebecca was seated at one end of the couch, while Peggy was in her usual spot in the only armchair. That left him with the choice of awkwardly sitting on the other side of the couch or choosing the rocking chair, which had been a favorite of Rebecca's when she was knitting mittens and hats from alpaca wool. He'd only started using the rocker recently, when he needed to calm Mackenzie down from an anxiety attack or rock her to sleep.

He and Rebecca had bought that rocking chair when they'd first started trying for a family, certain they'd be using it to rock their newborn within the year. How young and naive they'd been back then. Tanner never would have guessed that the desire to start a family could also ruin one.

When month after month the negative pregnancy tests taunted them, Tanner had subconsciously grown to despise that piece of furniture as a constant reminder of what had never been. And then after the stillbirth—

But at the moment, it was either the rocker or the couch, and he knew he would never be comfortable sitting right next to Rebecca. He settled in the rocker and took a sip of his coffee, welcoming the scald of hot liquid as it burned down his throat.

All three of them were looking at each other, but no one spoke. The tension and uneasiness was so palpable he could have sliced it.

How did one even start a conversation like this?

"So, Rebecca," Peggy said tentatively, relieving Tanner of having to be the first to speak. "Why don't you tell us what you remember."

What did she remember?

A big, fat nothing.

It was all she could do to remember what she'd had for breakfast this morning, although in the past month her short-term memory had made significant gains. It was impossible to describe how lost she felt. It was almost like someone coming out of a coma of many years and finding her life to be completely different than she recalled. She remembered her childhood up to a certain point and then there was nothing but a big, fat murky cloud shadowing her memories.

She'd returned to Serendipity in the hopes that seeing what ought to be familiar people and places would trigger her memory, but all she was getting was a throbbing headache for all her efforts.

She pulled out her cell phone and opened her notes. "My friend Dawn helped me with this," she explained. She didn't miss the resentful look that passed between Tanner and her mother. Neither appeared happy with the knowledge that the notes she was consulting came from Dawn.

Why was that?

"Is that who you've been staying with? Dawn Kyzer?" Mama asked, with a surprising edge to her tone that hadn't been there before.

Rebecca was startled by their negative reaction and responded a little defensively. Dawn had been her best friend all her life. She *remembered* that. Which meant her mother would have known that, as well. And though she didn't know the reasons behind the choices she'd made, she'd clearly gone to live with Dawn after her breakup with Tanner.

"I was driving, but Dawn was in the car with me when the accident happened. Thankfully, she only received a few bumps and bruises. She stayed by my side in the hospital and has cared for me ever since."

"Then we owe her for that," her mother acknowledged begrudgingly. "Although she should have called us and let us know what had happened."

Tanner didn't respond, but it was clear he didn't like Dawn. Rebecca searched her mind for why that might be, but no explanation came to her.

She was an amnesiac, but that didn't mean she was stupid. Dawn had obviously refused to come with her to Serendipity today, and now Rebecca could see why. There was some kind of rift between her husband and best friend, and she suspected she was the root cause of it. And her mother was right—Dawn should have reached out and let them know Rebecca had been in an accident instead of telling the hospital she was the only person Rebecca had.

Rebecca watched as Mackenzie carefully and methodically set up an entire ranch scene of stuffed animals, all the while humming a joyful tune under her breath. She positioned two horses, a cow, a pig, four goats and what Rebecca thought must be a llama in what Rebecca belatedly realized was with the same organization as Tanner's ranch. The little girl was brightly chattering away at the animals, making sure they knew they were in the right place and why. Rebecca couldn't help but smile as her heart warmed toward the preschooler.

Reluctantly, Rebecca turned her attention to the adults in the room.

"How long ago was the accident?" Tanner asked, gesturing to her ankle boot. "Tell us more about it."

She blinked in confusion and once again consulted the notes on her phone.

"It's been a month now. I was in the hospital for two weeks, the first of which in the ICU."

"Two *weeks*?" Peggy echoed. "Oh my."

"And your memory? It's not improved since then?"

"That's hard for me to gauge," she pointed out adroitly. "My short-term memory has its moments. I call it Swiss cheese. Sometimes I remember, sometimes I don't. I am having better success retaining an entire day's worth of memories, but they don't always follow me into the next day. I make copious notes about everything, mostly hoping to stimulate the fog in my brain. My long-term memory is completely AWOL ranging back to my early adulthood."

She paused. There was one question she'd been wanting to ask ever since she'd first encountered her mother at the community center. She had gathered her mom was staying with Tanner and helping with Mackenzie, but was that because—

"Mama?" Her voice was dry and she coughed to dislodge the emotions jamming her throat. "At the community center—I didn't see—didn't see—"

She couldn't finish her sentence as tears once again filled her eyes. At this point she couldn't seem to stop bawling and sniffling no matter which direction the conversation went. She pressed her palms to her eyes, not wanting to disturb little Mackenzie with a frightening outburst.

Her mother reached for her hand and gently stroked it in both of hers. "Your father passed away several years ago. He had a massive heart attack when he turned fifty."

"Oh, I—" Rebecca hiccuped and sniffled some more.

Tanner stood and reached for a box of tissues. He set the box next to her and pulled a couple out, handing them to her.

"Th-thank you. When I first saw you today," she said to her mother, "I had this flashback to you and Dad dancing in the kitchen."

Her mother laughed softly. She'd clearly had time to grieve and the memory was a pleasant one. "Oh, he was always doing that with me, silly man. He'd put a rose between his teeth and tango me from one end of the kitchen to the other."

Rebecca remained silent for a moment as the information and accompanying emotions washed over her. In her messed-up brain, her father had still been alive and well. To find out he wasn't—

Tanner cleared his throat. "He walked you down the aisle at our wedding."

Rebecca's eyes widened at the sensitivity of this man who was her husband. How could he know how important that would have been to her?

"He did?"

"You bet he did," her mother said. "I've never seen a prouder father than he was when he handed off his only daughter to a man he respected."

That man was Tanner—the man *she'd* chosen to separate from.

"You should have seen how nervous Tanner was when he came to your father and me to ask for your hand in marriage," her mother continued. "It was the cutest thing."

"Aw. Do you have to call me cute?" Tanner's cheeks

turned red. "Let's not go quite that far. Babies are cute. Puppies are cute. Cowboys are…rugged," he finished lamely.

Rebecca and her mom chuckled at his vain attempt to save his ego.

Privately, Rebecca thought Tanner was both rugged and cute. He had the rough skin of someone who spent all his time outdoors and worked with his hands, but the scruff on his face couldn't quite hide the twin dimples in his cheeks.

She looked back and forth from Tanner to her mother and once again changed the subject. There was so much she needed to know.

"Is Mackenzie…?" Her voice trailed off.

"Your niece," Tanner answered, sounding surprisingly patient given the circumstances. "My sister's girl. I'm her temporary guardian right now. If you had stayed—" He choked on the word and didn't finish his sentence.

They stared at each other for a moment without speaking. His gaze was saying so much, and yet there was nothing she could translate into words. She wondered if there might have been a time in the past when they *could* communicate that way, able to speak without words. At some point they must have been madly in love with each other. He'd asked her to marry him and she'd accepted, and she couldn't imagine marrying someone she didn't love with every fiber of her being.

So what had happened between the *I do*'s and today?

She wished she remembered what had broken them up. But maybe her brain wasn't ready to handle that much knowledge yet.

And yet it was the one question she most wanted to ask but was most afraid of voicing.

"So, you don't remember anything about—what? The last few years?" Mama asked. "You seemed to recognize me right away when we met earlier."

"Yes, but it wasn't exactly how you look now. Like I said, I get little flashes of memory sometimes, but they only serve to confuse me. I remembered you and Dad dancing. That's why I recognized you."

Once again, she consulted her notes on her phone. "My short-term memory is spotty. It's getting better every day, but I still occasionally forget things right after hearing or doing them. My amnesia appears to have completely erased several years of my life. The doctor says I will get better with time and that the best way for me to snap out of it is to immerse myself in the life I once knew, what's most familiar to me."

"I guess it makes sense then that you remember Dawn, who was your best friend since elementary school, and obviously you recognized your mom. But with me, you came up a complete blank, because I didn't come on to the scene until later on," Tanner observed bitterly.

"I'm sorry." She didn't know why, but she felt the need to apologize, even though none of this was her fault. But he sounded so *hurt* that she didn't remember him.

"Why'd you come back here?" Tanner asked, resentment rising in his tone. "Since you remember Dawn, why didn't you just stay with her?" She couldn't blame Tanner for his bitterness. They had been separated, so it was logical for him to ask why she'd search him out.

And she only realized as he asked the question that her presence here wasn't fair to him.

"Because my driver's license still says Serendipity."

"And your last name is Hamilton." It wasn't a question and Tanner didn't phrase it that way. He hadn't said *still* Hamilton. That made Rebecca more curious than ever as to what their relationship had been like before it had gone wrong.

Her gaze locked with his. "Yes. It does say Hamilton. But the person I remember is Rebecca Foster."

His brow lowered and his jaw ticked with strain.

"I'm here because this is where I have the best chance of triggering more recent memories, and at this point, I'd do anything to get them back. But I understand this isn't going to be easy for you. If you want me gone, I'll leave."

"Of course you won't leave," Mama exclaimed. "You have to stay with us. Let's not forget you and Tanner are about to have a baby together. Isn't that right, Tanner?"

Tanner continued to stare at her, his blue eyes sparkling with pain and anger.

Her breath caught in her throat as she waited for him to answer. Her whole world revolved around what he was about to say. If he sent her packing, which he had every right to do, how would she ever remember how things used to be?

But it really was his choice to make. It was his life she was barreling into after months apart, after who knew what had happened to tear them apart in the first place.

He blew out a breath and shook his head, an action that belied his next words.

"Yes, Rebecca. You should stay."

Chapter Three

Tanner stood in the kitchen, leaning against the counter and sipping from his mug of coffee as he waited for Rebecca to join him.

Because Rebecca had no recent memories and needed someone to look after her, it only made sense that she stay here at the ranch with him and Peggy.

But he didn't have to like it. In fact, it was ripping him up inside.

He didn't know what to do with his anger and resentment. It almost seemed unfair to direct his anger toward Rebecca under the circumstances, seeing as she remembered nothing of their lives together, never mind their breakup.

This woman wasn't the one who'd left him. And yet she was.

Even though they'd been separated and he'd had no real hope of reconciliation, his heart ached deeply that their whole relationship, every good and bad moment they'd experienced together, had just disappeared from her mind.

He had disappeared from her mind.

And now they were going to have a baby.

After everything, if God were gracious, they were finally going to see their dream come true.

Only now this special blessing was arriving in a crazy, broken world that Tanner had no idea how to fix. Not surprisingly, his gut ground with fear when he thought of this baby. Would he or she be healthy? He and Rebecca couldn't handle another heartbreak like the first one, especially now.

Adding his guardianship of Mackenzie to the mix just made everything that much more confusing—and that much more pressing. They had to figure out how to deal with all of their problems *now*.

Today, he was showing Rebecca around the ranch. He hoped maybe the familiar setting might trigger something for her. That's what her doctor had said.

Butterflies flitted around in his stomach. He had no idea why he was nervous. He'd been married to Rebecca near on six years now, even if they'd been separated for most of the last one.

It wasn't as if they were strangers. But in the oddest way, this almost felt like they were going on a first date. And for some reason, he really wanted to impress her with his ranch.

Their ranch.

He supposed it was because he didn't know how to act around her now. She was a different person from the woman he'd married, or even the one who had walked out on him six months ago.

He had to get to know *this* woman if they were going to get anywhere.

"I'm ready to go."

Tanner's heart leaped into his throat, hammering madly as he whirled around to see Rebecca enter the kitchen. He'd been so lost in his thoughts he hadn't heard her approach.

He swallowed hard when he got his first glance at her. She was wearing a cap-sleeved soft green T-shirt, formfitting blue jeans and sensible boots. She'd pulled her sleek auburn hair back into a ponytail and her copper eyes were glowing with anticipation.

One thing hadn't changed, and that was how beautiful she was to him. She was simply stunning. He couldn't help the way his heart always responded to her, now today just as it was then, from the day they'd first met.

Even if he didn't have any idea of the woman she'd become.

"Great," he said, setting his mug aside. "I'm anxious to show you everything. What would you like to see first?"

Her gaze went blank. "I don't know. I can't remember anything about the ranch. I barely know the names of the different kinds of animals, and that's only because my mind remembers what I learned in kindergarten more than college. Old MacDonald Had a Farm, you know." She chuckled dryly, but it wasn't much of a joke. "You'll have to show me around and explain just what it is you do here. I promise I'll take good notes."

He supposed that shouldn't have surprised him. If she didn't remember people, she wouldn't remember places, either. Or animals.

Peggy and her late husband, Casey, had both been schoolteachers and Rebecca had grown up in a house in town.

Becoming a rancher's wife had been a big adjustment for her, but she'd thrived on it. At least he'd thought she had, at the time. When they'd first married, she'd been excited about every little thing. After she'd plunged into a dark depression and wouldn't so much as get out of bed, he wasn't so sure. Maybe he'd never understood his wife at all.

"Let's start in the barn," he decided. Earlier that morning, he'd stabled her sorrel quarter horse mare, Calypso, so Rebecca would be able to see her and interact with her. He desperately hoped for a spark of recognition. She and Calypso had been inseparable from the moment he'd bought the horse for her as a wedding gift. Rebecca had ridden out every day after coming home from teaching school and had insisted on caring for the mare herself.

"Chicken coop's over there," he said as they walked toward the barn. "You used to gather eggs every morning before you went off to class."

"Really?" She wrinkled her nose in distaste and he could tell it wasn't ringing a bell. "I actually picked up eggs from under a chicken?"

He chuckled. "That's usually how it's done. Do you remember that you're a teacher?"

At this question she brightened up a little, her face coloring and her eyes sparkling.

"Middle school math. Try on this for weird and un-explainable. I still know how to do geometry and algebra. Even calculus and higher math. I might be able to go back to teaching at some point, as soon as I learn how to put names with faces again."

"Right." A cloud of discouragement formed in his chest. It seemed to him like she remembered everything *except* him. Was God punishing him for something? Because that's what it felt like right now.

They entered the barn and he hesitated, waiting to see if she would pick out Calypso from the five horses he'd stabled for his little test.

Rebecca walked from stall to stall, pausing to look at each of the horses. After a moment, she turned back to Tanner.

"They're all very nice," she said hesitantly. "I feel like this is all faintly familiar. Do I like riding?"

"Very much," he assured her. "You used to ride nearly every day. Do you have any idea which horse is yours?"

Her gaze widened and she shook her head.

"One of them is mine?" Her eyes lit with excitement and then darkened with frustration.

His heart dropped into his stomach. This must be incredibly traumatic for her. He couldn't even begin to imagine the stress she must feel. And here he was self-ishly dwelling on his own problems.

"You rode most afternoons after school to wind

down and clear your head. I thought you might recognize your mare. This is Calypso."

He led her to Calypso's stall and she opened the gate, sliding in next to her mare and running a hand across her neck.

"Hello, Calypso. It's nice to meet you —again."

Rebecca felt just the slightest flash of recognition after Tanner had introduced her to her mare. It was so short she couldn't grasp on to it and hold it, and she suspected it wouldn't have happened at all if Tanner hadn't outright told her which horse hers was.

She grabbed a soft-bristle brush from the wall and groomed Calypso, starting at her neck and working her way down. The act was both soothing and familiar. She hadn't remembered Calypso, but yet she instinctively knew how to take care of her. Tanner didn't have to tell her what to do.

"How do you know how to groom Calypso?" he asked. "You didn't start riding until after we were married. You can't remember anything about that time, or which horse is yours, but you know how to use a brush to groom Calypso?"

"I can't answer that," she said, putting the brush aside and affectionately running her hand down Calypso's muzzle before exiting the stall.

"There are certain things I know how to do, like driving a car or grooming a horse, but I can't remember people, or places—or specific animals, evidently. It must be some kind of muscle memory when it comes to doing certain things."

His gaze narrowed on her and studied her closely. She started to feel like a trained monkey in a circus. In a way, she was no better than that, performing acts she had no idea why she knew how to do but somehow just came naturally to her.

She locked her eyes with his so he'd know she wasn't lying or perpetrating some kind of elaborate hoax. Amnesia made no sense. The rules were that there were no rules. That was maybe what frustrated her the most.

"Let me show you the goats," he said. "Maybe they'll ring a bell for you."

The goats were up against the front porch and Tanner swept his hat off, waving it around to get the goats to disburse farther from the house. "Your little herd keeps the grass down around the house, so they aren't completely worthless. I don't ever have to bring out the mower."

"I like goats?" She watched a large black-and-white goat butting a much smaller tan one. It appeared to Rebecca like the larger was picking on the younger, and it made her wonder why she would want an animal like that in her yard.

Tanner grinned and nodded. "It was your idea to get them. You had to talk me into them. Mackenzie likes them, too."

Rebecca had reached the edge of the herd of goats and she hesitated, putting her hands in the front pockets of her jeans so she didn't have to touch them. They looked kind of mean with their little horns and slit eyes.

"Oh," she gasped, when one of the goats butted her leg, sending her off-balance. Tanner snaked his arm around her waist with lightning speed, steadying her until she could stand on her own two feet and back away. The bigger her son grew in her womb, the more klutzy and off-center she felt, like one of those penguins in Antarctica.

"It's okay," Tanner assured her with a chuckle. "He's just playing with you."

"What about that big one over there? It looks to me like he's picking on the little one."

"Naw. They're just playing."

Tanner had assured her that she liked goats. That he'd bought the herd because she'd asked him to.

And now they scared her and she wasn't sure she would ever find the guts to interact with them.

Everything frightened her. Would it always be this way?

"I've saved the best for last," Tanner said.

"There's more?" she asked, hoping he wasn't going to show her his cows. She didn't know how it had been in the past, but at the moment, she had zero interest in bovines. They had long tongues and licked their noses, and just—eww.

Now *how* did she manage to remember such inconsequential facts as those and yet was unable to remember she even had a husband, much less all the history between them? She was so frustrated she wanted to throw something, preferably something breakable.

He led her to the far side of the house where a small fenced pasture lay. Inside were fluffy creatures with long necks and enormous brown eyes.

"Llamas?" she guessed. It was one of those words

that just popped out from the back of her mind. She'd probably learned about llamas in elementary school.

Tanner leaned on the gate, but Rebecca held back.

"Close. That was a good guess. These are alpacas. This herd is not only your favorite hobby but your pride and joy."

"My...hobby? But don't they spit?" Another useless piece of trivia.

He laughed. His smile lit up his whole expression, softening the stress lines, and Rebecca's stomach did a little flip. She wished her response was from a glimmer of true recognition, but no. She couldn't go so far as to call it that.

It was physical chemistry. She could certainly understand why she'd been attracted enough to this cowboy to marry him. Even now, she found herself inexplicably drawn to him, though her brain refused to offer up why. He was handsome, and as he'd mentioned earlier, rugged, in a way that really captivated her.

"Alpacas spit sometimes. Llamas spit more often and they can be mean. Alpacas are for the most part gentle creatures. You use their wool to knit. You love everything about the whole process, from shearing their fleece to knitting hats and mittens for the homeless out of their wool. Do you remember how to knit?"

She nodded. She remembered how to knit, although she didn't recall knitting for the homeless. And she definitely didn't remember anything about the alpacas, nor any of the processes needed to turn fleece to knittable wool.

One of the alpacas spotted her and came at her at a

dead run. She gasped and stepped back, even though she wasn't leaning against the gate like Tanner was.

The alpaca screeched to a dead stop just short of the gate and chewed her out with the strangest honking noise she'd ever heard.

Tanner laughed. "They kind of sound like geese, don't they? Betty here is wondering why you haven't come to see her in so long."

"She looks like she needs a haircut," Rebecca said.

"Yeah. We'll have to do that soon if we're going to get you and your mom knitting in time for Christmas."

"Right." Rebecca hoped Tanner wasn't expecting *her* to do the shearing, although he'd said that was something she'd done in the past.

"A couple of years ago you started competing in agility competitions with the alpacas."

"Agility?" Not surprisingly, her mind was drawing a complete blank.

"Weaving through stakes, loading and unloading from a trailer, putting their packs on their backs. That sort of thing."

"I see." She didn't, of course.

"You're really good at it. You've won quite a few trophies. I don't know whether you noticed them or not, but we've got them all displayed on the mantel over the fireplace in the living room."

Rebecca's throat closed around her breath. Tanner almost sounded proud of her accomplishments.

Then his gaze clouded over and his frown deepened.

"After you left, I almost got rid of the alpacas," he admitted. "Keeping them around was just more work for me to do, and they reminded me of you on a constant basis. It—it was hard." He lifted his hat and tunneled his fingers through his blond hair, then replaced his hat and lowered the brim over his eyes.

Another alpaca, this one a spotted brown and white, approached the fence far less aggressively than the first one, and much less vocally, and leaned her head over, close enough for Rebecca to tentatively touch her soft wool.

"I'm glad you didn't sell them." Her throat tightened around the words. It was an odd feeling brushing her palm over the alpaca's soft head. She searched her mind and found nothing regarding the animals, and yet her heart naturally responded to their big brown eyes and enormous eyelashes.

Her baby gave her a good, swift kick in the ribs and she rubbed at the spot where his little heel was.

Tanner's gaze dropped to her belly. "Does the baby move around a lot?"

"Oh, yes. Come here and feel."

It was a little awkward taking Tanner's hand in hers and placing it over her belly, but the baby did a nice flip for his daddy, who grinned when he felt it.

There was something so special, so intimate, about a man and wife sharing this moment with their unborn child. She had lost far more than she knew, but somewhere deep down, one thought echoed through her heart and mind.

She was home.

Chapter Four

Tanner poured the perfect amount of waffle batter into the iron, closed it and flipped it over to cook. Knowing how to make waffle batter from biscuit powder was only one of the many things he'd had to learn after Rebecca had left him. He spread bacon evenly into a frying pan and grabbed an eighteen-pack of eggs out of the refrigerator, expertly cracking them one-handedly into a bowl.

After their wedding, his starry-eyed bride had taken over everything inside the house, from the cooking to the cleaning and laundry. She'd also done her fair share of outside chores. And worked a day job. She'd never complained, but after she'd left, Tanner had come to a belated realization that he really should have pitched in more and done his share of the inside chores, as well.

He glanced into the living room, where Rebecca was sitting cross-legged on the floor playing *ranch* with Mackenzie, making her stuffed animals talk in high, funny voices and deep, low ones. Mackenzie grabbed her tummy and rolled over, pealing with laughter as

Rebecca made the rooster ride on the horse's back, squawking wildly.

There was no sign of the depression which had shadowed Rebecca before she'd left Serendipity. Gone were the sadness and fatigue, the agitation and the way she'd pulled into herself and away from everyone and everything that used to have importance in her life.

Now she was contentedly sprawled across the living room rug making stuffed dogs bark and plastic cows moo.

And Mackenzie was eating it up. The little girl had lived her whole life in Denver and was completely enamored of the country lifestyle. She was becoming a regular cowgirl. No dollies or tea parties for this curly-haired sweetheart. Her world was all about horses, cows, goats, pigs, chickens and alpacas, and she loved every moment of it. She was even helping Tanner with minor chores around the ranch, learning the true meaning of what it meant to grow up in the country.

It was more than that, though. Rebecca was spending quality time with a little girl who'd had too little of that in her life. Though Tanner loved his sister, he wasn't blind to the fact that Lydia had never been an exceptional mother. She was too selfish, and usually too high, to give her daughter the kind of attention she needed.

Rebecca gave a lighthearted laugh and Tanner's gut tightened. She was so good with the little girl, a real natural. He had always believed Rebecca was meant to be a mother. It was part of what had attracted him to her in the first place.

That was why it had been so hard for him to believe the Lord wouldn't bless them with a child. Those three infertile years had been heartbreaking enough. And then when finally—finally—the pregnancy test was positive and their firstborn grew in her womb, only to be stillborn at seven months...

It just didn't seem fair. Why them? They believed in God, went to church every Sunday. Loved each other and were committed to being good parents and bringing their children up in the Lord.

He and Rebecca wanted—*had* wanted—a large family—four kids, at least. His sister, who was completely irresponsible in every area of her life, had, at best, looked upon her child as an inconvenience, during the time Tanner and Rebecca had remained childless.

After doing everything right, they had lost their child, while Lydia had given birth to a perfectly healthy little girl. Tanner struggled to find God's purpose in this when everything in his life was upside down.

And now Rebecca was pregnant again? It was so hard to remain positive when it seemed their whole lives had gone against them.

It was strange having Rebecca back in the house again, hearing her voice, her laughter. He couldn't help but respond mentally and emotionally to the woman he'd loved since the first moment he'd laid eyes on her.

And yet nothing was the same.

In the months after Rebecca had left him, Tanner had realized just how spoiled he'd become, relying on his wife to pick up the slack while he obliviously worked the ranch. There were so many areas of his life he'd never had to worry about, things Rebecca had quietly taken care of herself and never complained about.

He'd never thanked her or expressed his appreciation for everything she did. It had never even occurred to him that his dinner wouldn't be ready and waiting when he came in from the range every night. That his laundry wouldn't somehow be clean and neatly hung in his closet. That the horses wouldn't have been fed and their stalls cleaned out.

He scoffed inwardly. He'd been an idiot. He'd never been the romantic type. It wasn't his way to surprise Rebecca with flowers or chocolate in appreciation of all she did, not even on holidays. It was one of his many regrets.

After she'd left him, Tanner had subsisted on microwave dinners and sandwiches. Laundry had piled up until he didn't have a single clean undershirt in his drawer. He'd tried using the washing machine once, but as humiliating as it was to admit it now, he'd had no idea what all the knobs and buttons were for or what the labels meant and he'd ended up turning all his white undershirts and socks pink. He'd had to visit Emerson's Hardware, which also served as the town's clothing store, to buy more shirts and socks. He'd been afraid to run the washer again, sure he'd overflow the house with laundry suds if he'd tried.

He knew he ought to apologize to Rebecca right this second for the way he'd blindly ignored her contributions to the family. He ought to thank her for all she'd done for him over the years. But what good would that really do when she couldn't *remember* all she'd done back then?

It had been a double blessing when Mackenzie had come into his life, because soon after, Rebecca's mother, Peggy, had arrived at his door, suitcase in hand and a smile on her face. Without a shred of judgment in regard to Tanner's relationship with her daughter and not one word against him, she'd moved into one of the extra bedrooms and had taken over where Rebecca had left off, not only cleaning, cooking and caring for the house, but providing Mackenzie the stability she so desperately needed. That woman was a blessing on top of a blessing.

Tanner never would have been able to take care of the little girl on his own. There were still nights the small child cried for her mother. Peggy had known how to calm her, to sing soft lullabies and pray over her until the preschooler was lulled back to sleep. And by morning, Mackenzie was smiling and ready to greet the new day.

If only Tanner could do the same. What he wouldn't give to have the resiliency of a child. Every day was a new challenge stacked upon the top of all of the old ones. When things had started going poorly between him and Rebecca, even before she'd left him, he'd not often worn a smile. It wasn't until Mackenzie entered his life that she would occasionally coax a smile out of him, even sometimes a chuckle.

But in his heart he still grieved, even as, day by day, Peggy taught him to be more self-sufficient. He could cook a little now and he knew how to do his own laundry without turning everything pink.

"Who's hungry?" he called, serving up the scrambled eggs onto a platter. "I've got bacon."

"We can smell it from the living room," Rebecca said, inhaling deeply and smiling at Mackenzie, whose little hand she held. "I don't know about you, but my tummy is rumbling."

"Mine, too." Mackenzie looked up at Rebecca and patted her tummy, then smiled from ear to ear. "Uncle Tanner makes really yummy food."

"He does? Uncle Tanner can cook?"

Mackenzie looked up at Rebecca with sheer hero worship, and Tanner shared one of his rare smiles. It looked as if Rebecca had already completely won the little girl over.

"Bacon is my favorite," Rebecca continued, pushing Mackenzie up to the table and settling her with a napkin in her lap.

"Mine, too," Mackenzie immediately agreed.

"Mine, three," came another feminine voice from behind Tanner's shoulder. Peggy reached around him and grabbed a slice right off the platter he was holding, grinning as she popped the whole thing into her mouth. "You've really become a decent cook, cowboy," she said around a mouthful of bacon.

He raised his brow at the quasi compliment. "Gee, thanks."

The adults seated themselves at the table and Peggy held out her arms so they could hold hands around the table while Tanner said grace. Feeling Rebecca's soft hand in his, he could barely get the words out. Her other arm was still in a splint.

She hadn't talked much about the accident that had ultimately brought her back to Serendipity. Whether that was because she didn't remember it or she didn't want to share it with him, he couldn't say. But he didn't want to press her.

Right now, this second, she was happy. What was going to happen if—when—she got her memory back?

What if the darkness that had once taken over her heart returned?

What if she remembered why she'd left him in the first place and ran for the bushes?

Tanner choked on a forkful of eggs and swallowed hard.

"How does this memory-loss thing work, anyway?" he asked tentatively when he could speak again.

"How do you mean?" Rebecca gave him her full attention.

"Well, will you wake up one morning and it'll all come flooding back, or are you just remembering little bits at a time?"

"Or do you even know how it will work for you?" Peggy added, softening the blow. "What did your doctor say?"

Rebecca pulled out her cell phone, something Tanner was getting used to seeing her do. Anytime she needed to remember something she couldn't recall, she checked her list. Anything new that she learned as she went, she added to her ever-growing list.

"My doctor says my memory will come back in fits and starts," she said. "Or possibly all at once, though that is less likely. The more time I spend here doing what is familiar to me, the faster I ought to get better. But I don't know how long that will be or if I'll ever fully recover all my memories."

"You're welcome to stay as long as you need," he said without thinking, then paused and cringed.

What had he said that for? She was welcome to *stay*?

This was her *home* as much as it was his. Of course she could stay. She was welcome to stay forever—that is, if they could get over the current crisis and deal with their past marital concerns, issues which had once broken them apart.

"I appreciate that," she said, seemingly not realizing the huge gaff Tanner had just made—or purposefully choosing to ignore it.

"Is it possible you won't ever get your memory back?" Peggy asked gently.

Rebecca's eyes grew to the size of saucers. "I hope not. I can't imagine living this way forever. It's so frustrating. Paralyzing, really. I can't do most of the things I want to do, be the person I want to be."

"Like what?" Tanner asked, then berated himself for being too blunt. He'd always been that way. Words shot out of his mouth before they passed through his brain. It was part of the problem. He'd have to work on it.

He wanted to do better.

He did.

"Like riding my horse. I really want to learn how to do that again. Once I've had the baby, of course." She giggled, lightening the mood. "What's her name again? Or is it a he?"

"Calypso is a mare," he reminded her. "And there's no reason you can't go riding again once the baby is born. I wouldn't be surprised if you actually remember how to ride without further coaching."

"I think you might be right about that. It feels instinctive, although of course I won't know until I get in the saddle. But I'm sure to get lost if I take off on the land without knowing where I'm going."

"Not if I'm there with you," Tanner offered.

"Really? You'd take time out of your busy schedule to do that for me?"

Tanner wondered why it was that she thought he might not be willing.

Maybe because she knew she'd left him, even if she didn't know why. It was a wonder she was giving him this much latitude when she couldn't fill in all the blanks.

"Yeah. Of course," he assured her.

"My memory may come back before that, anyway," she said, rubbing the top of her belly. She smiled at Tanner. "He's kicking again. Do you want to feel?"

Tanner's heart jumped into his throat and then thunked down hard into his stomach.

"It's a boy?" he asked, tentatively holding his hand out to her. They'd talked about the baby, but it hadn't occurred to him that she might know the sex of the child.

She placed his hand over a bulge on her stomach and it moved. Rebecca helped Tanner press a little harder. He chuckled when the lump bumped back at him.

"Your son," Rebecca acknowledged. "I found out what gender I was carrying when I was in the hospital being treated after the accident. For some reason, that's one fact I don't have to check in my records every morning. I just know."

Tears welled in Tanner's eyes as he pressed his palm to Rebecca's belly. She hadn't expected that kind of reaction from the tough cowboy. What was he thinking?

He didn't seem like the emotional type. She didn't know why she thought that, but she was certain it was true. She wondered how much of that knowledge was mere observation and what, if anything, was innate, what her memory was providing her.

"A son," Tanner repeated tenderly, awe in his voice and expression. "And he's a strong little mover."

"Oh, yes," she agreed. "Soccer. Football. Something that requires a lot of running. Or flips. Maybe gymnastics or parkour." She paused and caught his gaze, gauging whether or not to ask the question. "This is okay, then, that we're having a baby?"

"This goes way beyond *okay*, Rebecca."

He paused and her gut tightened. His statement had been given in such a serious tone it could be read either way. Had he not wanted to start a family with her? Was this going to be yet one more issue they had to work out?

When his face split into a grin, she breathed easier.

"I've been praying God would bless us with a son or daughter since the day we said *I do*. You used to pray, too."

Rebecca's shoulders tensed so tightly that she couldn't turn her neck.

She *used* to pray? What did that even mean? Even with the amnesia, she hadn't lost her faith in God.

Tanner's sentence faded away into silence, leaving in Rebecca's chest a fiery ball of resentment and frustration. Why wouldn't anyone tell her what had happened that was so bad that she would want to separate from a man who, as far as she could tell now, was good and decent?

"Finish your sentence." She hoped she didn't sound

as exasperated as she felt, but honestly, she wanted to scream.

Rebecca's mom reached for her hand, but it was Tanner who spoke, his voice low and scratchy.

"We started trying for a family right after we got married. It—it didn't work out quite like we'd imagined."

Rebecca rapidly blinked back tears. She understood what he was saying to her. She couldn't get pregnant as they'd expected to be able to do. Was that what had eventually driven her away?

"Look. You have enough of a burden facing your present circumstances without bringing up the past. Let's focus on that," Tanner suggested.

"And you've got that lovely baby boy growing in your womb," her mother reminded her.

Maybe they were right. She had enough to worry about trying to face her future without bringing a past she couldn't remember into it. Perhaps they'd had a hard time conceiving, but now they had a healthy son growing in her womb. They should focus on that.

"How far along are you?" Tanner asked, eyeing her stomach again as if he wanted to reach out and touch it a second time. Even though she knew Tanner was the baby's father, it still felt weird to her to have him looking at her that way.

She sighed and checked her phone for the exact figure. "Seven months. Thirty-two weeks, to be precise. My due date is August eighteenth."

"Seven months?" Tanner echoed, sounding slightly alarmed.

"Yes. Seven. We've got about eight weeks to go before our son makes his debut. We probably ought to start thinking about putting a nursery together."

Tanner stared at her openmouthed for a moment. "What?"

He shook his head fervently.

"We need to get you in to see Dr. Delia as soon as possible so she can check you out," he said, even though Rebecca was well aware that wasn't what his look had been about. "She's the town doctor. I know you've been under a doctor's care, but I really trust Delia. Most of the ladies in Serendipity go to Mercy Medical in San Antonio and Delia delivers the babies. She's family practice and she's really good at what she does."

"That sounds nice," Rebecca agreed. "Are there childbirth classes in town?"

"I'm sure there are. I'll get us all signed up, okay? I—I mean, er, did you want your mom to be your birthing coach instead of me?"

"Is there any reason I can't have you both?"

"I—no—that would be great!" At least he sounded enthusiastic about coaching, though for some reason Rebecca pictured him as the kind of big, rugged father who would faint dead away in the delivery room.

"I wish I could remember everything we've gone through to get to this point," she said.

"Maybe it's better that you don't."

"You can't mean that."

He turned toward her, leaned his hip on the counter, crossed his arms and frowned. "No, I don't suppose I do."

"It's important to me to remember the bad times as well as the good. That's one thing I've learned through my memory loss. Life isn't just made up of the good times, but the bad, also. You can't know what it is to be happy unless you've been sad."

Tanner grunted in agreement. "Hold on just one second, will you? I have an idea."

She waited, curious, as he jogged to his bedroom—the one he and Rebecca had once shared—and returned with a wedding photo.

"This photo used to grace the mantel in the living room, but after you left me, I moved it to my bedside table."

She wondered why he had tortured himself that way, seeing Rebecca's happy face every morning when he rose for the day. That couldn't have been good. She was surprised he hadn't put it away in a drawer.

"I couldn't put it away," he said, as if he'd read her mind. "That would be like putting *you* away, and that I couldn't do. For me, marriage was until death did us part, even if my spouse didn't happen to agree with that vow."

"I'm sorry if I gave up on us, Tanner."

"I'm not sure you did. Not completely. We won't know until your memory returns. Anyway, here," he said, slipping the photograph into her hand. "This is us on our wedding day six years ago."

She stared at the picture for a moment, a smile lingering on her lips. "Now, this is something I'd *really* like to remember."

But would she? Even if she remembered why she'd left?

"We look so young," she remarked softly. "Young and madly in love."

More like foolish and in love. Two idealistic young

people who saw only good things in the future, who believed their faith would shield them from the many bumps and bruises of life. That a family was something that would just happen when they wanted it to. That their dream of a ranch and dog and at least four children sitting around the table at a meal would all come naturally.

Except it hadn't.

They didn't even have a dog—not even a working dog to help herd the cattle.

Rebecca gestured to the photo. "Would it be okay if I kept this picture for a while?"

He nodded and cleared his throat.

Rebecca slid the photo from the frame and placed it in the small purse she wore strung across her shoulders.

"I feel obligated to tell you we were separated at the time of your accident. Our lives didn't go anything like we imagined on our wedding day."

"I know."

He raised his eyebrows in surprise. "You *know*?"

She waved her cell phone in the air. "It's in my notes, although rather vaguely. I don't have all the specifics, and I know we'll have a lot of work to do when and if I remember what happened. But I couldn't just leave my marriage like that, and even though Dawn completely disagreed with me, as far as I am concerned, finding out we'd separated gave me all the more reason for me to come home."

Chapter Five

In the three days since they'd had that serious, heart-wrenching conversation over the breakfast table, Tanner inadvertently fell back into all of his old patterns, his way of dealing with hard things.

He subconsciously retreated to his ranch work, going out early and coming back late. Instead of manning up to his truths, he ran away and hid.

It was only when Rebecca caught him in the act that he realized what he was doing.

Before dawn on the fourth day, he dressed and went into the kitchen to make the coffee and pour himself a bowl of cold cereal before heading out to do his morning chores.

Rebecca startled ten years off his life when he flipped on the light and found her at the kitchen table, dozing quietly with her head tucked onto her folded arms, her auburn hair covering her face.

What in the world was she doing in the kitchen at this time of day—and sound asleep at the kitchen table, at that?

For a moment, he just stood silently, watching the peaceful rise and fall of her chest as she breathed. He hated to have to be the one to bring her back to the real world—a world full of challenges and stress.

"Rebecca, honey," he said, gently shaking her shoulder. "Wake up."

She mumbled something unintelligible and then shot straight up out of her seat, her eyes wide with shock.

"What's going on?" she asked, her voice high and tight.

"That's what I was about to ask you," he countered with a chuckle. "What are you doing sleeping in the kitchen? How long have you been here?"

"Oh." She yawned widely and covered her mouth with the back of her hand—a hand that was no longer in a splint. "I was waiting for you. I wasn't sure what time you got up in the morning, only that it was early, so I've been here since three a.m. I figured that way I for sure wouldn't miss you."

That sounded serious. He poured them both cups of coffee and slid into the chair across from her. His heart thudded as he waited for her explanation.

"Okay," he said, when she didn't immediately fill in the blank. "What's up that got you going so early this morning?"

"I know you're super busy with the ranch, and I don't want to bother you or take you away from that, but you're really the best one to show me what our lives were like before my accident. For years it was just the two of us, wasn't it? I've been hanging out with my mom and Mackenzie for the past few days, but Mom isn't that familiar with the ranch and Mackenzie is new to me, isn't she?"

"Mmm," he agreed, his throat tightening. "You're right. There's no reason you'd remember her. We went to her christening just after she was born, but then we didn't see her often. And you're right about your mom. She stepped in to help when I needed her, and she's been a huge blessing to me, but she wasn't raised on a ranch any more than you were. This is as new to her as it is to you."

He threaded his fingers through his hair. Once again, he had let Rebecca down. He hadn't been there for her after the miscarriage that he hadn't quite been able to find the courage to tell her about in their last discussion. He hadn't been there for her when major depression drove her into a darkness from which she could not be reached.

And now he had backed off and hadn't been here for her as she struggled to regain her memory. Or, apparently, when she'd visited the doctor to remove the splint on her wrist. And that after he had assured her that he'd been the one who would take her to see Dr. Delia.

"I'll do better," he promised. "So you saw the doctor, I take it?"

"Two days ago."

How had he missed that? Was it that easy for him to fall back into his old ways whenever stress hit?

"Yes. It was mostly about my splinted wrist. She says it's healed now, thankfully. I was really tired of wearing the splint all the time."

"Did you check on the—*our*—baby?"

She smiled softly. "Our son is right where he's supposed to be for this stage. He's got a strong, steady heartbeat and is just the right size." She reached around to the counter and picked up an ultrasound image, passing it to Tanner.

"That's his heart. His feet and arms. Here's the outline of his face. Isn't that the cutest little button nose you've ever seen?"

Tanner nodded, too choked up to answer.

"And look—he's sucking his thumb. He's already learned how to self-soothe. He's going to be the best baby ever."

Everything about that ultrasound picture was amazing. And that the baby had somehow come from God's blessing upon Tanner and Rebecca during the time they'd been facing such difficulties made it all the more special.

And all the more confusing.

"We should spend more time together, don't you think?" she asked. "Because of…" She gestured toward the ultrasound photo.

"Yes. The two of us need to get to know one another again. No matter how this amnesia thing plays out, I think it's important that we reestablish our relationship."

And hope for the best.

"I'd like to spend more time with you, but I don't want to be a burden to you. I know how busy you are with the ranch and I know I would just drag you down."

He winced. It wasn't being busy that had kept him from Rebecca's side the last few days. It had been his own confusion. He had made a vow to be faithful to her. Now it was time to put the past—a past he *did* remember—away and push his vow into action.

"I'll make time. This is important."

She bit the inside of her bottom lip and nodded. Tanner remembered she used to do that—nibble on her lip—when she was deep in thought about something. It was one of those gestures that made his gut flip.

"What?" he asked.

"I just don't even know where to start."

Tanner wished he could take Rebecca out on a horseback ride and show her their land and their prize herd of Irish Black beef cattle. He'd seen the way her eyes had lit up when they'd spoken of riding a horse again. Maybe she was experiencing some innate feelings deep within her that resonated when she thought about Calypso—that she instinctively understood how much she loved horses.

But that wouldn't work now. Though they could spend time with the horses, she couldn't ride. Not in her condition. So that would have to wait.

Those thoughts had, however, given him another idea, a way both to surprise Rebecca and hopefully stimulate more of her memories to return. It was a way to bring the whole family together, and if he didn't miss his guess, it would be fun for everyone.

"We could spend some time with your alpacas," he suggested. "Most of them are ready for shearing. That would, in a sense, be a new experience for all of us."

She smiled, her eyes glittering, and he couldn't help but grin back. This was the woman he remembered, the woman he'd fallen in love with so easily and who would always have his heart in her hand.

The woman *before*.

"Let me get my morning chores done and then we'll set up to shear one of them for practice. I imagine your mother and Mackenzie would like to join in."

"I'll help you out with the chores." Rebecca drank the last of her coffee and rinsed out her mug.

"You don't have to do that."

"You don't want me to help?"

Great. He'd hurt her feelings. That wasn't what he'd intended to do, but he somehow had to shake her for at least a little while.

Since Rebecca had always shorn her alpacas with her fellow alpaca enthusiasts' help, he had zero experience in how to do it. And Rebecca probably wouldn't remember how to shear an alpaca, unless it was one of those things that came back as muscle memory.

He intended to slip into his office in the stable and look up how to shear an alpaca on a couple of online videos so he could direct the process and not look like he didn't know what he was doing—even if he didn't know what he was doing.

But if Rebecca joined him with his chores, how was he going to slip away?

She shrugged when he didn't immediately accept her offer of help. "I don't mind. Really. Maybe you can show me what I need to do to care for the horses?"

He laughed. "Cleaning stables may be the least glamorous job on the ranch."

"But you said that used to be my chore, right?"

"I've gotta admit, I never did understand how anyone could think cleaning out stalls was an entertaining activity the way you always did."

"Well, me, neither, but the only way to find out is to try, don't you think?"

"I suppose so." She had a point. If nothing else, cleaning out the stable would be an *immersive* experience. "But I don't want you to feel you have to do it every day if you don't want to. Especially in your condition. And be careful with your wrist. You just got it out of a splint."

"I'll let you know how the experience goes for me," she promised, holding up one hand palm out. "But don't worry about me physically. I'm feeling much better now, other than having my foot in a walking boot. I'm extremely grateful to be past feeling nauseated in my pregnancy and am actually feeling quite well. I didn't have morning sickness. I had all-day sickness. But now I'm just always hungry, which I'll take any day over feeling sick to my stomach. And I'm doing better from the accident, as well. No more body aches and my wrist doesn't hurt at all. Now, if my memory would just heal…"

"Just don't overdo it," he said again.

They walked in silence down to the barn. Rebecca appeared distant, lost in her own thoughts, and Tanner didn't know what to say.

"We own six horses," he explained when they entered the stable.

To his astonishment, Rebecca walked straight up to her horse and offered her a carrot, stroking her neck affectionately. "Hello, Calypso, sweetheart."

"Wait, what? You remember which one of these is your horse—and her name?"

She turned, laughing when Calypso bumped the back of her head with her muzzle, clearly wanting all of Rebecca's attention focused on her.

"Okay, so I cheated and checked my notes this morning. But I have the oddest feeling right now that I would have remembered her anyway. I wonder if more of my short-term memory is returning?" Her smile widened. "Wouldn't that be great?"

This might seem like leaping over a small hurdle, but Tanner knew that to Rebecca, it was huge. She may have remembered something she'd been told within the last few days without using her cell phone notes. More than that, she'd remembered something important to her—her relationship with her horse, Calypso.

Tanner wanted to cheer, but that would freak out the horses, so he mentally fist-pumped instead.

Tanner now regretted the days he'd withdrawn from her. He'd been selfish and because of that had wasted important time. How much further along would she be right now if he'd been here working with her, stoking the fire of her memories back to life?

He was a coward. He knew why he'd returned to his old ways so easily. It was fear holding him back. He was afraid of what would happen once *all* of her memories returned and not just the short-term ones—when she remembered why she had left him. When she once again became aware of the pain of the miscarriage and all of the miserable months afterward and the depression she'd suffered through.

He wouldn't wish that kind of pain on anyone.

And could he help it if he didn't really want her to remember their separation? Things between them were so *good* now. He liked the relationship they were developing together. And yet from one second to the next it could all go downhill.

They were one memory away from disaster.

Tanner was billing the alpaca-shearing as a family event, but Rebecca wasn't so sure he was right. But of course he would be. He was the rancher. He knew what he was doing.

She'd been told—repeatedly—that the alpacas were *her* thing. She'd bought a couple of ebooks on the care and feeding of alpacas and the different types of performance events alpacas trained in, since Tanner had mentioned she'd once been interested in that. She'd spent a great deal of time out in the pasture, just taking quality time with the animals and trying to get to know the gentle creatures with the enormous brown eyes. They didn't frighten her anymore, although she wasn't sure she would ever not chuckle when one of them honked at her.

But no matter how she tried or how much time she spent, nothing permanent was sticking—in her mind, anyway. Her heart tugged whenever she was around her alpacas, suggesting how she used to feel about the animals.

It was so frustrating to continually have to return to her notes, not even able to remember just how many

times she'd done that very same thing—pull out her cell
phone and try to remember...

She dressed in a long-sleeved dark blue T-shirt, jeans
and cowboy boots. Her mom had taken her shopping in
Amarillo shortly after she'd returned home to get her the
clothes she'd need to work the ranch—maternity-style.

As far as the baby was concerned, she was starting
to look and feel like an elephant, lumbering around
with that particular large animal's pace—and with just
about as much grace.

She was the last one to reach the living room, where
the others were gathered and waiting for her. Darling
Mackenzie was bouncing on her heels, totally enthused
about spending time with Uncle Tanner and the 'pacas.
The outfit she'd picked out for the day—because she was
three and got to choose her own clothes now—included
pink jeans, a T-shirt with her favorite cartoon princess
on it and matching pink bows in her hair. At least Uncle
Tanner had persuaded her to wear her cowboy boots for
the excursion. It hadn't taken too much convincing, since
even her boots were pink.

"The whole herd needs to be sheared, but for today,
I think we ought to just start with one and see how it
goes," Tanner announced as they headed out the door.

One alpaca? The thought of what it took to shear
one of these animals overwhelmed Rebecca, but surely
Tanner was an expert. He'd spent his whole life on a
ranch. He was probably keeping it simple and sticking
to only one alpaca for her sake. She didn't really know
what to expect, but she imagined him zipping through
the whole herd with his shears and leaving a nice pile

of fleece at the end— wool which she would then somehow have to learn how to turn into yarn.

And knit. Let's not forget that she was eventually supposed to knit something out of the wool still currently
attached to the alpaca's backs. She *thought* she remembered how, but she hadn't yet put it into practice—and
there were homeless people depending on her for hats
and mittens at Christmas.

"Okay, then," Tanner said as they approached the
alpaca pen. "Who wants to pick out which alpaca gets
her haircut?"

"I do! I do!" Mackenzie exclaimed.

Having obviously expected that answer, Tanner
grinned down at his niece and held out his arms to her.

"Let's go take a look," Tanner said. Mackenzie
squeaked in excitement and crawled into her uncle's
arms.

Rebecca's heart warmed like hot tea with honey
watching Tanner with Mackenzie. He was exception-
ally patient with the little girl, allowing her to examine
each alpaca several times over, each time exclaiming
over the color of their coats, or the enormity of their
eyes, or how soft they were to the touch.

Eventually, Mackenzie settled on an alpaca she called
Brownie, which made sense, since the animal had a
light brown coat.

"He's pretty," Rebecca remarked.

"She," Tanner corrected. "This herd is all females.
You can't keep *machos* in with the *hembras* or you'll
have trouble."

"M-machos?" Rebecca repeated with a giggle, even

as her face heated from the error she had made. "The males are called *machos*?"

"Hey," Tanner said, pushing his chest out and flexing his biceps. "I think that's a great name for them."

Peggy snorted and Mackenzie burst into giggles. Even Rebecca had to smile at his crazy antics.

"So where are the—*machos*?"

"We don't have any. We use a stud service when necessary. You were really into researching bloodlines and were working on bettering your herd with every *cría* born. Conformity, color, condition of the wool. Everything fascinated you."

"It did?" At the moment, all of that information overwhelmed her. She couldn't imagine the amount of complicated data connected to pedigree research. She had enough to do just to remember all of her alpacas were girls.

She'd probably forgotten more than she'd learned, even if she'd spent the entire morning reviewing her notes. The alpaca herd had been her idea, so she felt obligated to take over that responsibility as soon as possible. She'd spent hours on video websites learning what she could about the animals, from the hay and fresh pasture they ate, which kept them full and happy, to who knew what else—she certainly couldn't remember many of the specifics right now.

"The first thing we have to do is catch her," said Tanner.

Rebecca had noticed that while the animals appeared docile, they sometimes skittered away when Tanner was near.

The goal, Tanner explained, was to get Brownie lying down and stretched out onto the tarp Tanner had fastened down just outside the alpacas' pasture. He'd placed removable wire fencing around the gate, making a holding pen of sorts to keep Brownie from bolting off.

"I'll go to the left," Rebecca offered.

Tanner nodded and jogged to the right. Peggy and Mackenzie stood next to the gate, ready and waiting to do their job of shooing Brownie into the holding pen.

First, they had to separate Brownie from the herd, which turned out to be not as easy as Rebecca would have imagined it might be. Brownie was determined to stay with her friends and nothing Tanner and Rebecca did appeared to make her want to change her mind on the issue.

Not being used to being around the alpacas—or any ranch animal, for that matter—Rebecca's heart was pounding as she inserted herself into the herd. She tried to be brave and not balk when the animals skittered around her. She somehow managed to get behind Brownie and shouted and waved her arms to usher the alpaca toward the gate.

It appeared to be working when suddenly Brownie veered to her left, where Tanner stood waiting with a halter in his hand. He waved his arm and hollered, but instead of turning toward the gate, the stubborn alpaca headed straight for Tanner, honking madly. Rebecca was certain she was going to head-butt him, but then at the last moment, she kicked up her hooves and made another ninety-degree turn to the left, dashing out to the middle of the field and the safety of the herd.

Tanner dove in front of her when she bolted, but all he managed to do was hit the ground and roll several times, raising dust in his wake.

Rebecca rushed over to him.

"Are you okay?" she asked, crouching beside the cowboy she'd once given her heart to. Whatever issues were between them, her heart had still jumped into her throat when she'd seen him fall.

He rolled to a sitting position and then crouched on his knees, taking a couple of deep breaths and coughing from the dust.

"I'm fine," he said, scowling. "The only thing that's hurting on me right now is my ego and my pride. I can't believe I let that critter get away from me."

He stood and brushed off his hat, jamming it back on his head and adjusting the brim.

"Maybe we should just choose whichever alpaca is easiest to pen," Rebecca suggested. "Is Brownie perhaps not one of the gentler animals?"

Tanner shook his head. "Mackenzie picked Brownie. Besides—that animal owes me something now. Brownie is getting sheared today whether she wants to or not, so she better just get it through that stubborn head of hers right now. Although from what I've read, this is the hard part and they feel much more comfortable once we get the thick wool off them."

"Read?" Rebecca asked, confused, but Tanner was already making his way toward the herd.

They chased the persistent alpaca around for several more unproductive minutes, whooping and hollering and laughing. Mackenzie was clapping with delight at the silly antics of her uncle Tanner and auntie 'Becca.

At one point, Rebecca's gaze met Tanner's and their eyes locked. He was clearly enjoying himself now and his brilliant blue eyes glittered as they met hers. He was a handsome, rugged man from the tips of his cowboy boots to the top of his dark brown cowboy hat, and her heart skipped more than one beat.

She might not remember her past with Tanner, but she could definitely see why she'd been attracted to him. The physical chemistry between them was undeniable, and for a moment, she chose to bask in the feelings rather than let them frustrate her, for one moment not caring about the rest of the story, whatever that was.

They were right here, right now, enjoying this experience between them. And this time, when they surrounded Brownie and herded her toward the opening, they managed to get her into the pen. They almost lost her at the gate, but with Peggy's and Mackenzie's added enthusiasm, Brownie darted through into the makeshift pen.

"Do you want to help Mackenzie put on the halter?" Tanner asked, extending the halter toward Rebecca.

She stepped forward with a self-conscious smile. Her heart was hammering, but she had this, right? She had reviewed the video on how to halter an alpaca just before they'd left this morning. She didn't quite remember *all* the details and the specific order of things, but really...

How hard could it be?

She took the halter in her hands, her confidence level

soaring, but when she picked up Mackenzie and they went to put the halter on Brownie, it took about two seconds for everything to go wonky. To start with, Brownie had no intention of being haltered and she wasn't about to cooperate. She stretched her neck and wiggled her head back and forth and it was everything Rebecca and Mackenzie could do to hook the loops around her muzzle and ears.

When Rebecca had finally captured the alpaca's head, she grinned in triumph, only to frown again a moment later.

The halter looked backward. Upside down, maybe? Inside out? Nothing fit where it was supposed to go.

It was incorrect and she knew it, to her chagrin. What she *didn't* know was how to fix it. Nothing suggested itself as an answer.

Tears of frustration sprang to her eyes. She understood what Tanner meant when he'd been talking about ego and pride raring up to the exclusion of all over emotions. She felt so useless. She couldn't even do a simple task like haltering an alpaca.

"Here, now," Tanner said gently, noticing her anxiety. "None of that, now. It was a good try."

She uttered something between a snort and a sniffle.

He placed his large, callused hand over hers and guided her as they turned the halter around and got everything where it needed to go to be appropriately placed on Brownie.

"There. See?" he said. "You've got it."

But she *didn't* have it. That was the point.

She'd watched videos a mere hour ago and any information she'd gathered was already history in her Swiss-cheese mind. An *hour*. She hated it when that happened, especially since she'd been making some good progress on her short-term memory.

But then there were moments like these. She didn't know what was worse—not remembering the last few years or what she'd eaten for breakfast.

Oh, wait. She'd forgotten to eat breakfast.

Tanner leaned close to her ear. "It's okay," he soothed. "No big deal."

She wanted to yell back at him that it wasn't okay and it was definitely a *big deal*, but none of this was his fault and it would be wrong to take it out on him when he had done so much for her.

He was every bit as patient with her as he was with Mackenzie, taking as much time as she needed to get things right.

Unable to voice her thoughts, she nodded her gratitude.

"Okay, so, Rebecca, you'll be catching the fleece as I shear it off Brownie here," Tanner explained. "As I mentioned, as I shear the blanket of wool off the back, it should come off in one long, even piece. That part is worth the most, so we'll bag it separately. I'll do my best to shear Brownie's legs and head, but no promises there on how it's going to look once I'm finished."

Rebecca had earlier pictured dashing after puffs of wool floating through the air and was glad to hear it wasn't as fanatical as all that.

But there it was again—the hesitancy in Tanner's voice. *No promises.* As if he didn't know for sure how this was going to go. As if he'd never shorn an alpaca before.

"How do we get her to lie down?" Rebecca asked as Brownie protested loudly with a sound somewhere between a goose's honk and a dog's squeaky toy.

"I've got that part all set up," Tanner assured her. With Rebecca keeping Brownie steady and speaking calmly to her, he carefully looped the alpaca's back legs and pulled them tight using a peg he'd nailed into the ground on one side of the blue tarp. "Okay, now, to get her down gently."

He reached for her front legs and managed to get the rope looped around them, but when he went to pull the rope tight and carefully roll Brownie to her side on the tarp, she turned her head toward him, and squealed in distress.

"She'll feel much better once the weight of the wool is off her," Tanner noted.

Peggy and Mackenzie settled near Brownie's head, petting her and talking to her to keep her calm. Rebecca organized her plastic bags, preparing to separate the wool as Tanner instructed.

Tanner oiled the enormous electric shears and away he went. Despite all he'd said—and not said—to the contrary, he was good at what he did. It showed that he'd worked with animals all his life. With a firm but gentle hand, he sheared the top wool off in a single, neat blanket and then sheared down to her knees and up her neck to her face.

Rebecca was duly impressed.

They rolled her over and Tanner finished the job on Brownie's left side, with Rebecca following just behind his shears to scoop up the soft wool and place it into plastic bags in order to keep it as clean as possible. Mackenzie very quickly got bored with the process and wandered off to play with the goats. Seeing that Tanner and Rebecca were doing fine on their own, Peggy soon followed Mackenzie.

"Okay, I think we can let Brownie up now," Tanner said, leaning back and pressing his palms into his thighs. "It's not perfect, but I think we got most of the wool."

Rebecca couldn't see that he'd made a single mistake and she told him so. It looked great to her, a real expert shearing.

"Really?" he asked, his shoulders squaring as ruddy color reached his tanned face. He graced her with a half smile. "This was kind of fun, wasn't it?"

"Yeah," she agreed. "It was. Except we have another nineteen alpacas to go. I hope we can shear more than one in a day next time."

"Practice makes perfect," he said, releasing Brownie's front legs. Without giving it a moment's thought, Rebecca took the now-calm alpaca's halter. Brownie looked much more comfortable not carrying all that extra wool on her.

"Hey, Mackenzie," Tanner called to their niece as he released Brownie's back legs. "Come see how Brownie's haircut turned out."

The sweet little girl was giggling even before she got to them. "Her neck is so skinny," she said. "And her head is so poofy."

Poofy was a good word for it. Rebecca had no idea how Tanner had managed *that* crazy hairdo, but Mackenzie started giggling harder, and before they knew it, all four of them were holding their stomachs from laughing so hard.

Tanner scooped Mackenzie into his arms and Rebecca led Brownie back to the pasture and released her halter, which wasn't nearly as complicated as putting it on. At least she was able to do that on her own.

"We work well together," she observed, even though in truth, Tanner had done most of the work.

Tanner's eyes widened. Rebecca nearly clapped a hand over her mouth when she realized what she'd said. There was still so much she didn't know—like why she hadn't been living in Serendipity with her husband when she'd been in her accident.

And yet what she'd said was true. They did work well together.

Should she ask for the truth, the whole truth and nothing but the truth?

But if she was just going to forget it again when she went to sleep that night, would it matter? More than likely, all she was going to do was bring up old hurts without a resolution and stir up Tanner's pain.

She didn't want to do that to Tanner. She *liked* the man. If she were being honest with herself, her feelings were beginning to run deeper even than merely liking him as a human being. They had a past together. They had, at one time, chosen to live out their lives together.

They were connected.

And she didn't want to hurt him.

Chapter Six

Tanner opened the gate to the chicken coop and laughed as Mackenzie burst inside, sending hens squawking in every direction, their tail feathers ruffling in indignation. He'd been Mackenzie's temporary guardian for going on five months now, but it never got old. His heart still warmed every single time he watched her play. She somehow drew everyone in and made them experience the same childlike joy she was feeling.

He wished he shared that capability. But if anything, he carried a rain cloud of dark and doubt over him—nothing he would want to share.

He'd sure miss her when her mama got out of jail and regained custody of the little tyke. Mackenzie belonged with her mother, of course, if Lydia could get her life together, but he worried that might not be the case.

It wasn't that Lydia didn't love Mackenzie. It was just that she didn't know *how* to love Mackenzie. She had made a mistake large enough to land her in jail—twice now. She wouldn't let him see her while in jail, much less Mackenzie, but she'd assured him she had changed while inside.

It was hard for Tanner to fathom not having the little girl here all the time. There would be a big gaping Mackenzie-sized hole in his heart when she was gone that even his own son would not be able to fill.

Today the preschooler was *helping* Uncle Tanner clean the chicken coop and gather the eggs.

Originally, Rebecca had wanted to help gather the eggs, but a quick internet search suggested chickens carried certain types of bacteria which might not be safe for the unborn baby. It seemed to him that she'd been rather less than enthusiastic about the chore to start with and appeared relieved to be able to immediately insist on putting their baby's health first.

He wouldn't have pushed her to do something she was uncomfortable with, anyway. In the weeks since she'd been back, they'd seemed to have found a nice middle ground in what chores they shared. And Tanner was finding it harder and harder to remember that she'd left him and he'd experienced that horrible separation when she was so very *present* now. The expression on her face as she did ranch chores—especially anything to do with the animals—was akin to Mackenzie's—all innocence and joy.

And there was something else that struck him as strange. She remembered her—*their*—baby without the least bit of prompting, although he supposed it would be hard to forget the baby even if she'd completely lost her memory again and woke up with nothing. She'd be aware of her living, moving baby bump from the very first second she awoke every morning. But she'd been extra cautious, like working out, all on her own, that she should wear gloves while doing ranch work. Her amnesia didn't remove her intelligence—it only blocked her memories.

Turning his attention to Mackenzie, he handed her a wicker basket and grabbed a rake to pull the used straw into a pile while she gathered the eggs. While Mackenzie hadn't been raised on a ranch until just recently, she had absolutely zero fear of animals. The very first time she'd gathered eggs, she'd reached right underneath one of the hens and had withdrawn her arm with a nice, fresh egg in her grasp. Talk about a natural-born rancher!

"Look at that," he said, admiring her basket as she filled it with eggs. "This is almost like an Easter egg hunt, isn't it?"

Mackenzie grinned and nodded vigorously.

"When's Easter?" she asked, excitement brimming in her gaze.

He laughed. Now he'd gone and done it.

"We just celebrated Easter a few months ago, remember? We went to church and all the bells were ringing? And if I remember right, the Easter bunny left you a big chocolate bunny and you ate the ears off."

Mackenzie clutched her middle and giggled so hard she nearly dropped the basket. "He couldn't hear no more."

"He couldn't hear *any* more," Tanner corrected gently.

She looked up and tilted her head at him, scrunching her eyebrows and pursing her lips. Clearly, she had no idea why he'd thought to correct her. Hadn't she just said exactly the same thing?

He shrugged and grinned and she broke out in another contagious bout of giggles that had him chuckling.

Uncles. What is a little girl to do with them?

Tanner was sure that's what Mackenzie was thinking.

"Why don't you take those eggs in to your grandma? I'll bet you can help her scramble some for lunch."

Mackenzie loved to *help* cook almost as much as she enjoyed gathering eggs, and wasted no time heading inside to her grandmother. Thankfully, Peggy was an infinitely patient woman where three-year-old little girls and cracked eggs were concerned.

Tanner finished raking up the chicken coop and spread some fresh straw across the ground. He scooped chicken feed and spread it so the chickens could enjoy scratching for it. Then he ran the hose in and filled up the water trough underneath the henhouse for the birds to drink and wash in.

He'd done this work all his life. Cleaning the chicken coop was the first ranch chore he'd been given when, as a small boy of about six, he went looking for work so he could put food on the table when his mother spent all her money on drugs. After all these years, he could perform the task effortlessly—and more to the point, brainlessly.

His thoughts kept returning to Rebecca, and his eyes often strayed to the alpaca field, where Rebecca was sitting on the gate with a notebook and pencil. She looked deeply thoughtful and he wondered what she was writing.

As for Tanner, his emotions were all over the map. He had to remind himself Rebecca had abandoned him. She'd touched his greatest vulnerability, that of being alone. He had experienced so much pain and grief as he'd adapted to life on his own. But as he thought on it, the stinging jab to the gut he expected to feel wasn't there—or at least it wasn't as obvious anymore.

He figured he ought to be hurting a good deal more than he was right now. He had enough reasons to be. He reminded himself to keep his heart guarded around her, especially until she recovered her memory. No matter how well they'd been getting along recently, the return of her memory could spell instant doom for their relationship, and he'd be wise to remember that.

Not only had Rebecca taken off without a word, but she hadn't even returned when she knew she was pregnant with his child. How irresponsible was that? He supposed she had tried to call him that one time and he'd hung up on her without allowing her to explain why she was phoning—presumably to say she was pregnant with their son.

That was on him—and he was ashamed of his actions. He should have let her talk and at least tried to listen to what she had to say. But that was one phone call. She was as much aware of his vices as he was and she of all people knew just how stubborn he could be. Was it fair that he believed she should have made more of an effort to touch base with him and share something that would change his world?

Why hadn't she made more of an effort to reconcile

with him—if not for their wedding vows, then at least for the sake of their child?

Or if not to reconcile, then at least to allow him to be the father he'd always wanted to be.

But then, their communication channels hadn't always been the best, especially after their daughter was stillborn. They weren't the kind of couple who pointlessly bickered back and forth. She withdrew into herself and he found his peace—or at least his space—on the range. But if her phone call *had* been all about the baby, then why hadn't she returned to town and faced him down in person so they could work it out together?

Maybe *together* was the whole problem. She'd clearly no longer wanted to be with him, or else why would she have left him?

Although yet another consideration was that maybe she'd been driving to Serendipity to share the news that she was expecting their baby when she'd been in the accident and had forgotten everything. That wasn't beyond a shadow of possibility, either. But until she regained her memory, they'd never know.

And yet here he was wondering if he really wanted her to get her memory back.

Realizing he was standing in the middle of the chicken coop gaping at his wife, he let himself out the gate and headed her direction. She was still focused on whatever she was writing and didn't hear him approach.

He glanced over her shoulder to see what she was working so intently on—only to find she wasn't writing at all.

She was drawing.

And she was *good*. She'd brought Brownie to life, funny haircut and all, with nothing more than notebook paper and a number two pencil.

"I didn't know you could draw," he murmured.

She jerked at the sound of his voice and her notebook and pencil went flying. She spiraled her arms and would have fallen backward off the gate had Tanner not been there to catch her.

"You scared the life out of me," she croaked, her breath ragged. "Warn a woman next time you sneak up behind her, will you, cowboy?"

At first he couldn't read her expression. For the first few seconds he thought she was mad at him, but then she smiled and his whole world turned right again.

They stared at each other in silence, his eyes locked with those gleaming copper pennies that had captured his heart from Day One. Tanner's breath was coming deeply as his gaze dropped to her lips, which were mere inches from his own.

Slowly, and with infinite gentleness, he lowered her to the ground, but didn't let go of her. She clenched her fists into the front of his shirt and tilted her head up, her breath warm on his cheek.

"Tanner, I—" she started, her voice lower than usual. It had taken on a husky quality that made Tanner's throat close around any answer he might have given.

He could no more stop himself from lowering his lips to hers than he could have stopped the sun from shining on this bright late-summer day.

He'd missed this. He'd missed her, more than he could possibly have realized until she was actually in his arms. It had been so long—far too long—for they had left nearly all closeness behind them the day Rebecca had suffered the miscarriage.

Now her rounded belly pressed into his and as they embraced each other, they embraced their unborn son, and Tanner felt truly blessed.

Rebecca ran her hands up his chest and around his neck, threading her fingers into the hair at the nape of his neck. A shiver ran through him. She used to do that—slide her hand around his neck, run her fingers through his hair and pull him closer. It was nearly choreography, and it felt so right.

He deepened their kiss. He might end up regretting this—he *probably* would—but for right here, right now, he had his wife back.

And that was all that mattered.

Everything about this moment was achingly and reassuringly familiar, tugging her even deeper into memories she could not quite recall. Tanner's arms, his warm lips, the sound which emerged from him as he pulled her closer and framed her face with his ranch-work-calloused hands.

Ever since she'd returned to Serendipity, she'd thought about what it would be like to be held in Tanner's arms, for him to kiss her, especially as her feelings for him continued to grow over the weeks she'd been at the ranch. How could she not be attracted to him?

And yet this went way beyond physical attraction. They had shared a life together, even if she didn't remember it. She was his wife. She'd fallen in love with him and believed they had a forever love. Otherwise she never would have married him. And she'd made a vow before God to be his until death did them part.

She closed her eyes and sighed as she leaned into his embrace. His thick blond hair was as soft as silk. Their kiss felt as natural as breathing. She *knew* this man, at a deep level that went beyond what her brain refused to supply.

And yet there was something about being here with Tanner that felt brand-new. In some ways they felt like different people. Rebecca sensed it wasn't just her amnesia at play here.

There was more.

Like why she'd left. Tanner clearly still cared for her, didn't he?

Had their separation been all her fault?

She didn't know, and from the feelings she was currently experiencing, she couldn't even begin to guess. She wished she could just get her brain to stop trying so hard and simply enjoy the moment. But the angst and confusion these thoughts brought with them caused her fight-or-flight instinct to kick in, a whole new surge of adrenaline that had nothing to do with sharing a kiss and everything to do with—she didn't even know.

And there was the rub. Even though she trusted Tanner and had wanted this kiss as much as he had, she couldn't let this happen.

Not until she remembered…

"No," she murmured into his lips, pressing her palms to his chest. "Tanner. No. We've got to stop."

He immediately dropped his arms and stepped back, gazing at her in confusion through desire-filled eyes.

"I— What?" His voice was like gravel. "What is it, Rebecca?"

"I don't know. I don't think—"

He jammed his hands into his pockets and chuckled dryly, without mirth, almost a scoff. "You weren't supposed to be thinking."

"No. I know. I—I'm feeling what you're feeling, Tanner."

His eyebrows lowered into a scowl. "Then why...?"

"You *know* why. I need to be sure. Until I have my memories back, I have to tread carefully. I don't— I can't—" she stammered.

She turned away from him and picked up her now-dusty notebook and pencil. She would do anything not to have to look into his eyes, which were glittering with pain and rejection. And it was just that much worse knowing she was the one who'd caused this mess. Her heart felt like it was going to rip in half.

"When you walked up to me—you said you didn't know I could draw?" she asked in a desperate attempt to change the subject and move forward onto safe ground. Her heart was still hammering and her pulse was racing from their encounter, and she imagined it must be much the same for Tanner.

They needed a moment, and she was doing her best to provide it.

He shook his head and then lifted his hat and pushed back his hair with his palm.

Rebecca's mind flashed back to——*something*. It was only a second, and then it was gone.

Another time. Another place. The exact same movement he'd just made. She *recognized* this tell. She had seen it before, knew what it meant.

He was frustrated. Ready to protect his heart—the heart *she'd* broken—by backing off a bad situation.

Was it a memory?

"What's wrong?" His gaze lingered on hers.

"I— Nothing." She wasn't ready to share this experience with him. Not when she didn't know what it was. She pulled her notebook to her chest in an unconsciously defensive gesture.

"Yeah—that drawing is amazing," he said, tapping his hat against his thigh. "You really caught Brownie's essence. I can even see the sparkle in her eyes. What made you think you could do this?"

"I—I don't know. It was just there. I found a blank notebook on the desk in your office and had the overwhelming urge to draw something. I hope you don't mind that I took it without asking."

"No. Not at all. Strange, though, that you'd have this much talent when I didn't even know you liked to draw."

"I didn't, either. Of course, I don't know much of anything these days." It was a bad joke, and neither one of them really laughed.

"It just seems weird that I wouldn't know you had artistic tendencies. It seems like the sort of thing that would be out in the open with a couple who share their lives together. I wonder if it has something to do with your amnesia? Do you think hitting your head might have changed your likes and abilities?"

She shook her head. "That's too weird to think about. I'm me, but I'm not me. And my brain learned to draw without my cognizance?"

"Yeah. That is kind of Twilight Zone-y."

She sighed and brushed a palm over her forcaim as if a chill had just gone through her.

"Hey," he said, reaching out a hand to caress her arm. "We'll figure it out together, okay? You're not alone here. Your amnesia brought you back to me. I'm not taking that blessing lightly. When we got married, we told each other it was you and me against the world. It still is, Rebecca. We may have nothing but new waters ahead of us, but God brought you back to me, and no matter what happens, whether we're facing the future or the past, I'm not going to lose you again."

Chapter Seven

Tanner snapped down his Sunday-best white Western shirt and tucked it into his best jeans. The Lord's day was his favorite day of the week, when he could put all his worries and ranch problems aside and just worship God. Being a rancher, he still had daily chores to do that didn't take Sundays off, like feeding all the animals, but he still always made it a point to attend the church service and whenever he was able, he caught an afternoon nap.

Today was the first Sunday Rebecca was accompanying the family to church. It wasn't so much that her amnesia had wiped out all memories of her faith. Her belief in God was one of the few things she appeared to have retained. But she hadn't been ready to face her friends and neighbors until now.

Tanner dolloped gel into his palm and ran it through his hair, trying without success to tame the thick, unruly waves. Not that it really mattered. His cowboy hat would ruin any attempts at tidying his hopeless mop of hair.

He hadn't seen Rebecca since yesterday's fiasco. Kissing her was singularly the very best—and the very worst—thing he could have possibly done. He was afraid he'd said too much, that in expressing his feelings to Rebecca, he would chase her away for good. But he'd wanted to let her know she had his support. He knew amnesia was frightening and he wanted to make sure she knew she wasn't alone in this.

Their kiss had rocked his world. In some ways, it felt like the very first kiss they'd ever shared together—the one at a Christian singles mixer on their college campus, where his heart had spoken to him and he'd known beyond doubt that Rebecca was the only woman for him.

He still believed she was. Even time, distance and the way she'd ripped his heart out with a razor when she'd left had never changed that. And as he'd said to Rebecca yesterday, he was incredibly grateful to God for bringing her back to him, even with her Swiss-cheese state of mind.

But he was scared to death he was going to lose her again once her memory fully returned. What would happen then, when the truth came out? Would she feel he'd been lying to her by what he'd neglected to tell her? Would she make a beeline out of town, and out of his life?

They'd built a new relationship between them in the weeks she'd been back, between two people who'd been changed by what had happened to them in the past. Was it possible they'd be able to work through the emotional mess that had once made her feel she'd had no choice but to leave him?

"Tanner?" Peggy called from the living room. "You done gussying up in there? We're going to be late for the service."

He jogged out to the living room and slammed to a halt when he saw Rebecca standing there, as beautiful as he'd ever seen her. She was wearing a white sundress dotted with bluebonnets and had added just enough makeup to make her eyes glisten like the brand-new copper pennies they were.

Their eyes met and locked. *This* was the woman he'd been married to for so many years? She literally took his breath away. He'd forgotten just how beautiful she was.

He wanted to compliment her, but his voice didn't seem to be working. He couldn't seem to be able to get the words in his head to come out of his mouth.

"Stop gaping, sweetheart," Peggy teased, tapping Tanner underneath his chin with the tip of her forefinger. "Just tell her she's pretty and let's be on our way."

"I— You—you look pretty," he stammered.

Rebecca's cheeks turned a bright pink that clashed with her auburn hair.

"What about me?" Mackenzie demanded. "Am I pretty, too, Uncle Tanner?"

He laughed and crouched down, opening his arms to the child. She jumped into them and he stood, swinging her around until she giggled.

"You are the most beautiful girl in the world," he assured her.

"Yes, indeed you are," Rebecca agreed.

As they loaded up in Peggy's 4x4, Tanner noticed

Rebecca's expression, an odd combination of excitement and anxiety.

This couldn't be easy for her, he realized, not recognizing everyone who'd known you all your life. Everyone would be so excited to see her that they might very well overwhelm her. He'd have to be on guard for that and gently but firmly remain in control. He met her eyes in the rearview mirror and smiled encouragingly.

Rebecca held back when they reached the church. Wide-eyed and breathing heavily, she looked as if she were ready to bolt. Tanner couldn't blame her. It took a lot of strength for her to be here.

He reached for her hand. "You don't have to do this today if you're not ready. There's no rush. I'll drive you back to the ranch if you want."

She stared at him for a long time before answering.

"No. I think I *do* need to do this. I don't know if or when I'll get my full memory back again, but I've been making what I think are some major strides with my short-term memory."

She had? Why hadn't she mentioned that before?

"As soon as I open my eyes in the morning, I remember my baby—our baby—is a boy. I've been able to recall Mackenzie's name and that she's our niece without referring to my notes, although I still have to work through why she is staying here with us to keep that part fresh in my mind."

"That's awesome. Do you remember anything about—about—"

She shook her head and he breathed a sigh of relief.

"No. Nothing long-term yet. But maybe meeting

some of the people I've known all my life will help stir my memories."

"Okay, then. I won't leave your side." He threaded his fingers through hers as they walked into the church building.

The first part wasn't so difficult, as they'd arrived just before the service started. They slipped into a pew near the back of the sanctuary and while there were a few curious stares, most everyone was concentrating on worshipping God and the service passed in peace.

Afterward, everyone moved into the fellowship hall to share coffee, donuts and hot, fresh breakfast burritos being sold by the children's choir to raise money so they could take a tour to sing in Italy the following spring.

"Do you want a donut or a burrito?" he asked.

"A maple donut. Yum squared!" She didn't even blink before answering.

He stared at her.

"What?" she asked apprehensively, and then she groaned. "Don't tell me. I hate maple donuts and love spicy breakfast burritos?"

He shook his head. "No, actually. You're spot-on with the maple donut. Those were always your favorite. Do you think it's a memory?"

She shrugged. "Hard to say. But I still want my donut."

He grinned and gestured to a chair. "Is it okay if I leave you here for a bit while I get our donuts and coffee?"

Her eyes widened and she swallowed hard, but she nodded. "I'll be fine."

"I can find your mom if you want."

"Don't bother. I see her over there. She's talking to her friends."

"Yeah. The altar guild."

"I don't want to interrupt her."

Tanner had to admire her courage. They both knew that the moment Tanner stepped away, she'd be deluged by her friends and neighbors who'd known she left town—and Tanner—and even more attention-grabbing, had heard the rumors about her amnesia. Everyone probably had a million questions to ask her.

"I've got this." Jo Spencer appeared out of nowhere and bustled her ample frame into the chair next to Rebecca. "Your wife and I have some catching up to do."

His *wife*.

She *was* his wife of six years. So why was that so hard to hear? Why did it feel so different? Why did his heart hurt?

Because this—the way they lived now, in peace and harmony with one another—was all a lie?

He glanced at Rebecca to see her reaction to Jo's words but she had a sweet smile on her face and didn't flinch, so he left her in the elderly redhead's kind hands and threaded his way over to the table to grab the coffee and donuts.

As he'd anticipated, by the time he returned, Rebecca was surrounded with friends welcoming her back to town—and to church—and everyone was anxious to find out how she was faring.

"Amnesia is tricky. I may have to ask you your names a thousand times, so please don't be offended if I don't immediately catch on," Rebecca joked, and those around her laughed. "But if you're patient with me, I'll get there eventually."

"We heard you were staying at the ranch with Tanner," one man said, his voice full of skepticism.

"Of course. He's my husband. Where else would I be?"

At her question, the crowd around her slipped into a silence that deadened the air in the room. Tanner couldn't breathe, and he doubted many of the others around him were able to, either.

Could Rebecca fill the sudden chill that had settled over the fellowship hall because of her words?

It was time to fly to her rescue as he'd promised himself he would do. He shouldn't have left her even to get donuts and coffee. What had he been thinking?

He placed the donuts and coffee on the table and moved around to stand behind Rebecca, gently massaging her shoulders to let her know he was there to support her.

She placed a hand over his and gave it a gentle squeeze, silently letting him know that she was aware of his presence and they were in this together.

He couldn't protect her—not in the way he wanted to. People would think and say whatever they desired and there wasn't a thing he could do about it. But he would do what he could to douse the flames.

"Rebecca is getting reacquainted with her old life," he explained. "Her doctor thought coming back to the ranch, where she lived—" He paused and coughed to clear his throat before continuing. "...during the majority of her adult life, might help jump-start her brain so she can regain her memories."

"And you're good with that?" the same nosy neighbor queried. "This doesn't bother you at all?"

"Now, Elliott Jacob Myers," Jo said, using the grown man's full name in a voice that would rival any mother of a troublemaking child who'd climbed a tree and scraped his knee. "You know perfectly well that kind of talk is just plain rude. Apologize to the Hamiltons this instant."

Tanner supposed he really shouldn't have been surprised that Elliott immediately followed Jo's orders.

The middle-aged man tipped his hat at Rebecca, looking chagrined. "Sorry, ma'am. Jo is right. Didn't mean to hurt your feelings." And then to Tanner he said, "I apologize. Sometimes my mouth goes faster than my brain."

"That's okay," Rebecca replied magnanimously. "It's nothing I haven't thought of myself. It's all rather confusing."

"But it's absolutely none of your business," Jo reminded Elliott, although her gaze scanned the entire crowd in warning. Clearly, she was speaking to everyone, and from the expressions on the congregation's faces, they understood the message. "It's our God-given responsibility to hold up our dear brother and sister in the Lord as they work through this unusual trial. And not just in prayer, either, although of course prayin' is a great place to start. Hold out your hand in friendship and see what you can do to help them along. God didn't give each of you a unique calling and graces for nothing, you know."

Frank Spencer, a crotchety old man who was the

polar opposite of his wife, Jo, and yet who somehow managed to make their marriage work, snorted at his wife's remark.

"We already had one sermon today, missus. We don't need to hear another one from you."

Jo chuckled. "Like you would know. You dozed throughout most of the service."

Tanner couldn't help but laugh. He'd give anything to have the kind of relationship those two feisty seniors shared. When he'd stood at the altar with Rebecca and promised his heart and his life to her, he'd thought that married life would be so much easier than it had turned out to be. Sure, he'd known there would be ups and downs, but he'd imagined that, like Frank and Jo, he and Rebecca would have been able to work out their problems in love.

That hadn't happened.

And everyone in this room—barring Rebecca— knew they hadn't ended up happily ever after. And even she suspected.

Which was why his fight-or-flight—preferably flight— instinct was raging inside him, screaming for him to take Rebecca's hand and flee for the ranch.

He probably would have suggested leaving, but at that moment, Rebecca reached for his arm and asked him to help her haul herself to her feet.

"Goodness," she murmured, placing a hand over her belly, "I never imagined it would be quite this awkward."

"I'm sorry. I should have thought—" he started, before realizing she wasn't talking about the awkwardness of being in the fellowship hall with dozens of people she should know but didn't.

She was talking about her pregnancy.

Her gaze widened on him. "Sorry for what?"

He shook his head. "Nothing. It's nothing."

"Good, then. Why don't you be a dear and introduce me to everyone. I've got a lot of catching up to do."

It was rather overwhelming, trying to put names to faces when everyone knew you and you couldn't remember anyone.

She was glad to have Tanner by her side, his hand linked with hers. His touch settled her nerves and made her believe in herself—her lumbering, awkward, big-bellied self.

"You were such a math geek in high school," one of the five women in a group she'd gone to school with was telling her. Apparently, they'd all been close friends back in the day, but had drifted apart some as they'd gotten married and started families. They felt familiar to her, but they'd changed so much her mind simply wasn't making the connections.

"And that was a bad thing? Being good at math?"

"You were—different," admitted another of her friends, whose face she could not put a name to. There were simply too many people in this room to figure one from the other, so she'd quickly stopped trying. Right now her mind was tagging them Bleach Blonde, Blondie, Brunette and Silky Black based on their hair colors. She realized she rounded out the five with her fiery auburn locks. "The rest of us were cheerleaders or we marched in the band, while you tortured—I mean *tutored*—other kids in calculus. You're a genius, you know."

Rebecca's first inclination was to snark back that she didn't know, but she kept her mouth shut. It wasn't her friends' fault her brain was Swiss cheese. It was just that sometimes, like now, everything she didn't know frustrated her to no end.

And they thought she was a genius. She couldn't even remember what day it was.

"Do you remember that you were a middle school math teacher before you...left?" Silky Black stuttered a bit at the end of her question.

Rebecca nodded. "I understand they filled my spot without too much trouble. I don't remember the particulars, but I know I wouldn't have wanted to cause them any trouble. And I don't blame them for finding someone to replace me. From what I hear, I left them in the lurch. And though at the moment I can't imagine myself being that irresponsible, the facts speak for themselves."

No one had anything to say about that statement and a sense of awkwardness settled heavily over Rebecca. Her mouth was getting her into trouble. Maybe she should just stay quiet until she could remember what, exactly, those facts were.

Tanner squeezed her hand and winked affectionately. "Breathe," he mouthed, reminding her that she could only do what she could do.

She gave her best shot at a smile, though she knew her lips were quivering. "That's okay, though. I really have a lot of work to do helping Tanner on the ranch.

If I have time, I may think about taking in some high school students to tutor on the side."

"You remember calculus?" one of the women asked in amazement. "No way!"

"You do ranch work?" queried another at the exact same time, with an equal note of astonishment in her tone.

"I—er—yes. Oddly enough, I remember everything about higher math. I can do complicated equations without second-guessing myself. I have no idea why or how I know. I just do. I also apparently know how to draw, which is something, according to Tanner—" she paused and tipped her head back to smile at him "—is something I didn't do before I got T-boned by a truck."

"Fascinating," the brunette said.

"*Strange* is the word I think you're searching for," Rebecca said. "Weird."

"We don't think you're weird," Blondie assured her. "You've been through a huge ordeal with the accident and all. We're all praying your memory returns soon so you can get on with your life."

Rebecca felt Tanner's hand tighten around hers—almost painfully—and she wondered if he even knew he was gripping her hand with so much force.

"Tanner is patiently helping me learn all the ins and outs of how our ranch is run. I want to contribute as much as I can to our bottom line." She shrugged. "I find most of it fascinating, and I wouldn't be able to do any of it without him."

She gently removed her hand from his. He grimaced as he belatedly realized he'd had a death grip on her hand.

"Really?" asked one of the women. "You are seriously spending your days out working on the ranch and getting your boots muddy?"

"Boots, jeans, shirt and hat," she assured her friends. "One thing that's firmly in my shiny-new memory—ranching is a dusty business."

"Yes, but, Rebecca—you're...um...*very* pregnant. And still recovering from the accident. Do you think it's a good idea for you to be out doing heavy labor?"

"Oh, it's not like that. I'm careful. I'd never do anything to harm our baby. But the fresh air does the baby and me good. And trust me—Tanner watches me like a hawk. He's always making sure I don't overdo it. He treats me like glass, as if I'm going to break at any moment."

That statement caused a strange reaction among her friends. Wide-eyed, they surreptitiously glanced at each other—and at Tanner.

He set his jaw and moved closer to Rebecca, resting his palm on the small of her back. His message was loud and clear—they were a couple. And if anyone wanted to argue the point they would go through him.

Rebecca wasn't sure how she felt about that. There were too many variables she had yet to discover. But for the moment, she appreciated Tanner's gesture so she didn't feel quite so alone in her awkwardness.

"Hmm," Brunette said, shaking her head. "I can't see it."

Tanner frowned. "Can't see what?"

"You may not know this about her, Tanner, since you moved to Serendipity as an adult, but back in high school, Rebecca was the one voted to be the most likely to really make something of herself."

"She has," Tanner stated in a flat voice.

Bleach Blonde waved away his protest. "That's not what we mean at all. It's obvious she's happy with you and Mackenzie and a baby on the way. And—from what we hear—doing ranch work." She chuckled at her own joke. "But you well know Rebecca didn't grow up on the land, with her parents being teachers and all. She was a walking, talking advertisement for women in STEM. We all thought she was going to leave Serendipity to go study at Massachusetts Institute of Technology or somewhere and never come back."

"But then I met Tanner, right?"

"Then you met me," he agreed. "And apparently, I changed the whole vector of your life."

He sounded miserable. Could this be part of the reason they had separated? Had she resented him for not allowing her to pursue her passion—whatever that was? She couldn't imagine anything that would be more fulfilling than loving on Mackenzie and feeling her son kicking within her womb.

And that was nothing to say about how her congested mixture of emotions for Tanner grew with every day they spent together.

"Granted, the five of us grew up together and we all married ranchers, too," Silky Black said. "That's kind of what women do in Serendipity. But, Rebecca, I don't recall you ever having any love for the great outdoors, especially when it comes to chores with smelly animals. I know I, for one, stay out of the pigpen and let my husband, Chris, do all the dirty work at our ranch."

"I think our pigs are kind of cute," Rebecca said with a chuckle. She was teasing, of course. They didn't even have pigs. But it was totally worth it to see her friends' reactions.

Her friends might be thinking she was kind of strange, but she, in turn, thought Silky Black was the weirdest one of the five. If, as she'd said, they had all grown up expecting to marry ranchers—and not only that, but she suspected most of them had been raised on ranches themselves—one would think they would be more than prepared to be ranch wives, ready to pitch in and help their husbands find success on the land. She knew that's what she wanted to do for Tanner.

And though they hadn't actually sat down and talked about it, she expected their son to do his fair share of ranch chores when he was old enough to do so—to learn the business from his father. To learn to love the land and the animals.

Tanner had already made it a point to include Mackenzie in ranch work, and she was only three. He was going to be an amazing father.

"Our son will grow up working the ranch beside his father," she said, catching Tanner's gaze.

She didn't have a clue what he was thinking, but he pulled the brim of his hat lower and swallowed convulsively.

"Our niece, Mackenzie, is three, and she absolutely loves doing ranch chores—feeding the goats, gathering the eggs from the chicken coop. We even sheared the alpacas."

"Now, I *do* remember your obsession with alpacas," Bleach Blonde said. "If someone wanted to get you talking, that was the way to do it. You called them your babies."

Rebecca felt as if Bleach Blonde's sentence had skidded to a halt, even though she'd finished it. Her pale skin definitely colored a bright red and Rebecca wondered what she was thinking about.

Tanner didn't seem to notice. "They're still very much her babies. Although with us taking care of Mackenzie now and with our son arriving soon, I suspect she has other babies on her mind, as well."

He placed a protective hand on her belly and their son walloped him with a good, swift kick. Tanner looked at Rebecca and they broke out in laughter.

"He's moving around a lot," Tanner said. It sounded to Rebecca almost as if he was reassuring himself. She supposed that was the great thing about being the mother—she could always feel her unborn baby. But Tanner had no reason to worry.

"He's practicing to play sports with his daddy," she said, her heart swelling with warmth. "Or maybe he'll be a black belt in karate. He's definitely got his kicks down."

Rebecca didn't miss the way the ladies shifted and glanced at each other.

What had she said?

Every time she started to feel comfortable in a situation, something like this would happen and her awkwardness and stress would return in spades.

"It's past Mackenzie's nap time, so we've got to run,"

Tanner said, sliding a firm arm around Rebecca's shoulder. "We'll see you all next Sunday."

As they made their exit—or rather, their escape—Tanner tilted his head down and whispered in her ear, his tone laced with concern. "Too much?"

She thought about it for a moment before shaking her head. "No. It might have been, but I was fine since you were there with me."

And that was the truth. Alone, she would have been lost.

But she felt safe with Tanner beside her. She was beginning to rely on him to be her rock and her shield.

Even so, she still didn't know what she didn't know.

And that scared her now more than ever, now that she knew how very much she had to lose.

Chapter Eight

Tanner had always been an early riser. Ever since he was a kid, rushing off to do chores for the neighbors so he could bring in a little money, he would pour himself a bowl of cereal, douse it in milk and make quick work of it so he could get outside. He'd never liked being cooped up inside. It made him antsy not to be able to breathe fresh air and see the sky above him.

He didn't know who his father was and Lydia's father had skipped out as soon as he'd heard Tanner's mom was pregnant. After she'd had Lydia, she'd turned to drugs to get through her days. His mother had never been a strong woman. Tanner had tried to protect Lydia, but he'd just been a young boy himself and felt he'd failed her—which was one of the reasons taking care of Mackenzie was such a priority for him.

He would not fail Mackenzie.

He decided against cold cereal and poured himself a second cup of coffee. He had changed in the past few weeks that Rebecca had been here. Suddenly, he wanted to be wherever she was. He hadn't been this twitter-pated since the time he'd first met Rebecca at the state college, where she was getting a degree in higher math and education and he was learning agribusiness.

Tanner had wanted to be a rancher ever since he was a little boy, but she was the reason he'd bought a ranch in Serendipity. His life had all come together when he'd met Rebecca. He loved Serendipity and having his own ranch.

It was their home.

Tanner opened the refrigerator and pulled out eggs, bacon and Texas toast. He was going to surprise the family with bacon, scrambled eggs and French toast this morning. It was Rebecca's favorite—or at least, it had been. She'd even make it for dinner sometimes.

Now—it was hard to say. He supposed this was yet another kind of experiment, to see if her tastes had changed along with her sudden ability to draw. She'd liked maple donuts just as she had way back when, so he thought French toast was probably a reasonable choice.

He was humming to himself when Rebecca entered and brushed her palm over his shoulders.

"Smells delicious," she murmured, pecking his scruffy cheek.

He closed his eyes and breathed in deeply—partly because of her familiar sweet scent and partly because, probably without realizing it, she'd just performed an intimate, loving action she'd done hundreds of times throughout their marriage. Or at least, before things had gone sour between them.

He wondered about her perfume. Had she brought it

with her in the small backpack she'd carried in that first day? Or had she bought it somewhere along the way, instinctively knowing it was her—and his—favorite?

"Sit down and relax," he said, reaching for a mug to fetch her a cup of coffee. "Breakfast will be ready soon."

"Tanner?"

"Hmm?" He turned and wiped his hands on a dish towel.

"You don't have to try so hard. You're spoiling me rotten, when you've got your own work to do. You don't have to hover over me. I'll be fine."

His throat clenched. Was that what she thought he was doing? Hovering over her?

"I'm sorry. I'm not trying to be annoying."

"Oh, there's nothing to apologize for. I'm just afraid I'm taking you away from what you need to be doing. You do important work around here. Not that I won't gladly eat that delicious French toast you're cooking up for us. It smells delightful."

"I'm not hovering because I don't trust you," he tried to explain.

"What is it, then? Are you afraid I'll get myself into a pickle with my Swiss-cheese brain?"

He laughed. "You don't have to have amnesia to do that. You were always the one to feel for the underdog. You got yourself into more trouble trying to help. People, animals—it didn't matter. You follow your heart. That was one of the things that most drew me to you when we were first dating."

His face heated as their eyes met and locked. She was searching for something in his gaze. But what?

"Can I be honest?" she asked.

"Always."

"Yesterday, at church? I felt like we were a couple. There was more than that, of course. I owe you big-time. I would never have gotten through all those introductions and everyone's reminders of the things I'd done in my past had you not been there with me. But it was more than that. I felt…connected to you."

His throat constricted even more and he fought for a breath. He blinked against the haze in his eyes, refusing to call them what they were.

Tears.

Because he felt the same way.

He was falling in love with his wife in a brand-new way.

He nodded. "I know what you mean. I—feel the same way."

"We have to tread carefully if we want to try to work on the possibility of building a new relationship. I don't know about you, but the whole thing frightens me to death. I don't know what is going to happen where my memory is concerned. It could come back in bits and pieces, or I might remember everything all at once. I can't imagine anything more overwhelming."

Tanner was gutted. She had no idea *just* how overwhelming her memories would be—but he had no doubt they would change everything.

It might be better for him to put a stop to this here and now.

Tanner placed the platters of French toast, scrambled eggs and bacon on the table and sat down opposite Rebecca. It wouldn't be long before the smell of bacon brought Mackenzie running, and Peggy would be along soon afterward.

He reached his hand across the table and took Rebecca's.

"This is uncharted territory," he admitted. "But I want you to know that no matter what has happened to us in our past, my love for you never wavered. Not even when we were having problems. Not even when we were—" He had trouble pushing the word across his lips. "Separated."

"I wish I could say the same," Rebecca admitted. "I'm sure I was in love with you. I know I was. Honestly, I can't imagine anything that would cause me to run away like that, to ignore my wedding vows to you. What happened, Tanner?"

His heart dropped straight into his already mangled gut. He broke his gaze away from her, let go of her hand and threaded his fingers through his hair. This was the moment he had dreaded since the second Rebecca had returned to his life.

Because *he* knew why she'd left.

"Oh, Lord, guide me," he whispered.

What was he supposed to do now?

Their relationship was developing, their feelings for each other growing stronger with every day that passed and with all the time they were spending together.

Why couldn't they just move forward the way things were currently?

But he already knew the answer to his own question. With the amnesia still a barrier between them, their relationship was incomplete. A couple grew together—or further apart—because of what they went through together as they faced life as one. Even though Rebecca couldn't remember the years they spent together, *he* could. And that was a ravine that couldn't be crossed. Not until she regained her memory.

And when that happened, when she knew the chasm that lay between them, only God knew where they would go from there.

But their history together, even the bad parts—was what made their relationship genuine and long-lasting.

He hated this. By not saying anything, he was living a lie.

He studied her, wondering what, if anything, he should say.

How did he tell the woman he loved more than life itself that after three years of infertility, she had gotten pregnant, and had carried their precious baby nearly to term, only to have their joy turn to anguish when the baby was stillborn?

How did he explain holding their unbreathing infant daughter in their arms, their hearts crushed beyond measure?

Rebecca had the right to know the truth, but was she strong enough to hear it? With her amnesia still plaguing her, would it even do any good to tell her the whole story? Or would it just cause her unnecessary pain?

It was only recently that he'd been able to make peace with his wife and with God.

And the next words out of his mouth might ruin everything.

* * *

Rebecca tensed, sensing Tanner was going to rock her world, and not in a good way. His expression was one of sheer agony, and he didn't even try to bother to wipe the tears from his eyes.

Whatever was wrong had broken their marriage apart then, and she was terrified it would do so again.

And he wasn't the only one who had some sharing to do. She hadn't yet admitted that many of her memories were returning. At this point it was just small bits and pieces, and most of them were out of context, but they were significant enough that she felt Tanner should know about them.

Last night as she'd lay curled on her bed staring at their wedding picture, flashes of memories—at least, she thought they were memories—assaulted not only her brain, but all of her senses. She could *feel* her love for Tanner, her excitement about their lives to come. She even remembered the scent of the woodsy cologne he was wearing that day.

In her mind's eye, she saw the look on Tanner's face as her father lifted her veil, kissed her cheek and then presented her to Tanner, placing her in his care. Tears had flooded down her face. Tears of happiness and joy at having found the love of her life.

Tears of sorrow that her father had passed and she couldn't remember.

But there was more—and these memories weren't quite as clear or forthcoming. Her heart and mind strained to understand what she was feeling. Grueling emotions of heartbreak and bitterness. A loss so deep there was nothing but a gaping hole where her heart used to be. Pain so intense it bit right through her like frostbite.

Yet that part of her existence was nothing more than feelings, vague emotions which, no matter how hard she tried, she couldn't attach to anything she knew about herself. She searched her mind but found nothing concrete.

No memories. Just feelings.

Her life here, now, was so full of joy and happiness. She had a family. Tanner doted on her. The feelings budding in her heart for her husband were tangible and authentic—the total opposite of the way things must have been between them for her to abandon him and leave.

She needed Tanner to fill in the gap between what she knew and felt and what had actually happened between them.

"Please," she practically begged. "Tell me what happened to me—to us."

He cleared his throat. "Rebecca, I—I don't even know where to begin."

"The beginning?" she suggested. "The only way we are going to get through this is if we are 100 percent honest with each other."

"I agree." He clenched his jaw so tightly Rebecca could see the pulse beating in the corner.

He took a fortifying sip of his coffee. "Okay, then. We were young when we married and completely in love with each other, but though we were mature for our age, we were, frankly, more than a little naive about how our lives were going to go. We only saw the good stuff. I suppose we talked about what life would look like when we faced challenges, but we were so in love I think we believed love itself would conquer all wrongs."

"If only," Rebecca murmured.

Tanner nodded. "We wanted to start a family right away, right after our honeymoon was over. Even that seems crazy now—we planned to have five or six kids and figured we ought to get right on it."

"Five or *six*?" Rebecca echoed, stunned.

One side of Tanner's lips lifted into a half smile. "I know. Crazy, right?"

"That's one word for it."

"The thing is, it didn't happen. We were surprised when the months came and went and still no baby. It seemed so easy for other couples. They decided they wanted to get pregnant and it happened for them right away. We had always assumed it would be the same for us. We had no idea just how difficult it could be—or how much it would affect our relationship."

He took a sip of his coffee. "The first year or so, we weren't overly worried about it when you didn't get pregnant. We had other things on our minds, trying to adjust as a married couple. We were busy figuring out what married life would look like for us—what life in general would look like, really. We'd just bought the ranch and I spent every waking hour working to get it up and running. You'd taken a position teaching advanced math at the middle school. Given our frantic lives, we just assumed it might take some time before we got pregnant. We trusted God for His perfect timing.

"Which was easy, at first. We enjoyed being together as a couple and our marriage hadn't yet been hit by any of life's unexpected tornadoes. Everything was perfect between us."

Rebecca raised her eyebrows. "Perfect? You really thought our lives were perfect?"

His throat tightened. "Why? Didn't you?"

"You know I can't answer that question. But nothing is perfect. Not in real life. And clearly things went south between us at some point. I can't imagine that we just woke up one morning and *bam*, everything was wrong and I could no longer stay here with you. For me to believe separation, even a temporary one, was the only answer— there must be a *much* bigger explanation for that."

Tanner just shrugged.

"Surely we fought sometimes, worried about how we'd make ends meet, that sort of thing. Bickering, at least. I know I'm not perfect in that regard."

He threaded his fingers through his hair. "Well, sure. We occasionally sniped at each other when we got overtired, just like any other normal young married couple. But not a lot, and we always made up with each other before the sun went down on our anger. That was one of our relationship rules."

"That makes sense, since it's in the Bible. Tell me— how did that work out in practice?"

"We allowed each other to leave the room to cool off and get our heads together. Then we always came back and talked our problems through, no matter how big or small the matter was. We always worked it out right away."

"You said we had guidelines. What were the other ones?" she asked curiously.

"To love and respect each other—always. I'm the first one to admit I wasn't always good at that. I tend to back off when I should be stepping up. It's always been an issue for me. It's easy to lose myself in the ranch when I should be manning up and facing my issues."

"And yet *I'm* the one who left."

Tanner grunted in assent. "Yes. But I didn't appreciate you as much as I should have—or at least, I didn't vocalize my appreciation. So it's not all on you."

"Was there anything else?" she asked. "Any other special promises we made to each other when we got married?"

"Only one. We made a rule never to use the word *divorce*. Not even joking, and especially not when we were angry with each other. For us, divorce was not an option, so why even put it out there?"

"That's sensible." Rebecca had thought she sensed bitterness lining Tanner's tone when this conversation had started. Now she knew for sure he was hurting. And it killed her that she was the one who'd broken his heart.

But there was one more thing she had to know, even though it would very much be throwing fuel on the fire.

"Once the D-word is out there, you can't take it back, even if you don't really mean it," she said softly. "So did I?"

Tanner's blond eyebrows lowered over his eyes, which had darkened to the color of twilight. "Did you what?"

It was time to put it out there, the question she'd been mulling over ever since she'd arrived in Serendipity.

"Tell you I wanted a divorce?"

He looked away from her and crossed his arms, his breath coming heavy. He didn't say anything for the longest time. Finally, he switched his gaze back to her, his jaw tight with strain.

"No."

She let out the breath she hadn't even realized she'd been holding. So she hadn't asked Tanner for a divorce.

Thank God. Oh, thank God for that small mercy.

"And yet I left."

He nodded.

"I broke our rule not to let the sun go down on our anger."

He shook his head. "Not exactly. That ship had sailed months ago. By the time we separated, we weren't even talking to each other."

"So that's why I left, then? Because we weren't talking?"

He shrugged and shook his head violently. "How should I know? I came in from work one evening and you were gone. You didn't even leave a note. I had no idea where you went. I tried calling but you'd turned off your phone. I had the whole town looking for you."

"That seems so…not like me," Rebecca murmured. "Why wouldn't I leave a note to tell you where I'd gone? If nothing else, in case of emergency."

Could she really have done this to Tanner? What kind of woman was she?

She had to wonder.

"I don't know," he said. "But you weren't quite yourself at the time. You'd sunk into a deep depression because—"

"Uncle Tanner!" Mackenzie exclaimed, bolting into the room at the speed of light and launching herself onto Tanner's back, then squeezing her arms around his neck until he looked as if she was choking him.

His expression immediately changed to one of joy and happiness as he stood and gently took her hands in his to save his air pipe, adjusting her grip so he could breathe.

"Be my horsey, Uncle Tanner," Mackenzie demanded, wiggling closer to him and wrapping her legs around his waist. "Giddyap, horsey!"

To the preschooler's delight, Tanner snorted and whinnied and then took off at a gallop around the house.

Rebecca's heart was racing as fast as Tanner's legs. He was so good with Mackenzie. She could easily imagine him with their son. Tanner was born to be a father.

But there was still something serious in their relationship which had yet to be repaired.

What had he been about to say?

She couldn't even begin to guess. But the moment had been broken, and who knew when they'd find the right moment to be able to have such a serious discussion again.

Maybe her memories would return on their own.

Only now, she wasn't sure she wanted them to.

Chapter Nine

Making sure he had a good hold on the little girl, Tanner bucked and snorted and trotted all around the house. He loved playing horsey with Mackenzie. Her delighted laughs and squeals made his day. He was glad he could do something to bring the little girl joy when she'd been through so much sorrow. No child should have to be without their mommy, as he well knew.

Now that he thought about it, it was about time for Mackenzie to learn how to ride a real horsey. Rebecca, too, once she'd given birth. She'd expressed to him on more than one occasion that she couldn't wait to be able to explore the ranch on horseback.

Although riding lessons might not even be necessary in Rebecca's case. She might very well remember how to ride Calypso without any prompting on his part. She'd been an expert rider before her accident. It was one of those weird Swiss-cheese situations he didn't really understand and couldn't begin to second-guess. She remembered how to do things like drive or cook or do upper-level math equations, but couldn't remember her own husband's face—nor why they'd broken up.

Their conversation this morning had gone well into the deep territory he'd hoped it would, but they had been interrupted before Tanner had gotten to the worst part—the truth that might send Rebecca running for a second time.

He snorted and whinnied and headed back for the kitchen so Mackenzie could eat her breakfast, but before he reached the alcove where the kitchen table was located, the doorbell rang.

Frowning, he twisted Mackenzie around to his front side and plopped her into a kitchen chair.

"Expecting anyone?" he asked, glancing from Peggy to Rebecca.

Both ladies shook their heads.

"Hmm. Me, neither."

He strode toward the door in consternation. Maybe it was a neighbor or one of Rebecca's old friends come to call.

"Ms. Goodwin," Tanner said in surprise as he opened the door a crack. It was Mackenzie's social worker, and she hadn't called ahead.

Tanner was immediately worried. What had Lydia done now? Or was the woman here to see how he was faring with Mackenzie?

He widened the door so the diminutive yet poised woman could pass by. "Please, come on in."

"It's Terri," she corrected him, and then, upon seeing the rest of the family in the kitchen alcove, said,

"Oh, I'm terribly sorry. I didn't mean to interrupt your breakfast."

"Not a problem," Peggy said. "Would you like to join us? We have plenty. French toast, bacon and scrambled eggs."

"No, thank you. I ate earlier. I wouldn't say no to a cup of coffee, though."

Tanner had followed Terri into the kitchen and gestured for her to take a seat at the table. He reached for a mug, filling it with the steaming brew and placing it before their guest—although Terri wasn't exactly a guest in the typical sense of the word.

She was a social worker. Mackenzie's social worker.

Terri had a smile on her face as she glanced around the table and opened her file folder, quickly browsing its contents.

"Is everything okay with my sister?" Tanner asked, his pulse hammering.

"Actually, I am here to talk about Lydia. But first, how are you doing, Mackenzie? Are you having fun with your uncle Tanner?"

Mackenzie giggled. "He's a good horsey."

Terri smiled softly. "I imagine he is. I see you are doing a good job eating your French toast."

"French toast is my favorite," Mackenzie told Terri, her chubby face turning serious. "My uncle Tanner makes the best French toast in the whole, wide world."

Terri flashed a glance at Tanner and smiled. "My. That's some praise, coming from a three-year-old."

"Mackenzie, would you like to go help me feed the goats?" Peggy asked enticingly.

The little girl looked from Peggy to Terri and then back again. It was a tough decision—a stranger visiting at the house was a rarity and her curiosity was clearly tripped.

But then again—*goats*.

Thankfully, in the end, the goats won and Mackenzie left without complaining, leaving Tanner and Rebecca to converse with Terri.

"It looks like things are going very well here with Mackenzie," Terri said as soon as they were alone.

"As well as can be expected under the circumstances," Tanner answered honestly. "She still occasionally has her moments when she has bad dreams and calls out for her mommy in the middle of the night."

Terri nodded. "Unfortunately, that's to be expected. It's heartbreaking, I know."

"Rebecca has a special touch," he said. "She always manages to rock Mackenzie back to sleep within minutes, whereas when I didn't have her help, it always took me much longer than that."

Terri eyed Rebecca for a moment and then put out her hand. "I'm Terri Goodwin, Mackenzie's social worker."

"I figured," Rebecca said. "As Tanner mentioned, I'm Rebecca. Tanner's wife."

"Wife?" Terri asked, her confused glance resting on Tanner. "But I thought—"

"It's complicated," he answered.

"We've reconciled," Rebecca said, totally stunning Tanner, who suddenly felt as if he'd just been run over by a rabid moose. This was news to him. I mean, he'd hoped, but...

"Mackenzie has a nice, stable home here," Rebecca assured Terri.

Tanner's head was spinning and he tried to suck in a breath, but it was a no-go. He raised a silent prayer thanking God for Rebecca, who was putting all of her own questions and worries aside for Mackenzie's sake.

And she wasn't wrong about their household. Things with Mackenzie had much improved since Rebecca's arrival. Rebecca had a mother's heart and seemed to know just what Mackenzie needed, often before the little girl did.

Best of all, Tanner didn't feel quite so alone in raising Mackenzie. Of course, Peggy had been there for him since Day One, even going so far as to move here to the ranch with him, and he was so, so grateful for all she had done, but their lives since Rebecca had arrived were a whole other thing entirely.

Rebecca had brought back the sunshine.

Terri studied her notes, looking as if she was trying to figure out a tactful way of asking her next question. "You weren't—uh—*here* before."

Tanner cringed. The last thing he wanted to do was get into the multifaceted complications of their relationship. Even worse, he worried what might happen if and when Terri learned of Rebecca's amnesia. What if Terri thought Rebecca might be a danger to Mackenzie because of her condition? Tanner was 100 percent positive she wasn't, but how would he convince Terri of that?

Would Tanner be presented with the impossible choice of keeping Mackenzie or losing Rebecca?

Rebecca didn't wait for Tanner to answer. She caught

Terri's gaze and held it tightly as Tanner looked on breathlessly.

"I'm here now."

Only three little words, but spoken with so much strength and confidence that Tanner wanted to stand and applaud her. He was shaking inside and just short of trembling on the outside, but Rebecca was as cool as a cucumber.

"While the circumstances are far from ideal for Tanner's poor sister," Rebecca continued, her voice unwavering, "Mackenzie has brought great joy into our lives. We've been blessed to have had the time to get to know her better." Rebecca smiled widely and pressed a hand to her belly. "And she's been great practice for when our son comes along."

Terri's gaze dropped to Rebecca's stomach. "I didn't realize. I guess congratulations are in order."

Tanner was sure Terri was wondering why he hadn't mentioned such a monumental piece of information, but he wasn't going to enlighten her. Saying he hadn't known his wife was pregnant would be opening Pandora's box and there would be no way to shut it again.

"Thank you," Rebecca answered for both of them, her voice calm and steady. "Needless to say, Tanner and I are thrilled to be expecting our first."

Tanner cringed, but he was the only one in the room who knew that statement wasn't quite accurate.

"Will this baby interfere with your guardianship of Mackenzie?" Terri asked bluntly. "I don't mean to sound insensitive, but some families don't care to have guardianship of other children once they have their own. I would rather just ask the question up front."

"No," Tanner barked, then took a breath when he realized how harsh he sounded. "I guess you have your reasons for asking, but Mackenzie is a member of this family, every bit as much as our son. She'll stay with us until my sister is well enough and strong enough to be a mother on her own."

He realized he was making his sister sound as if she was ill and not in jail, but in Tanner's mind, that's how he thought of her. If it hadn't been for their upbringing, his sister would not be in this position now. She wouldn't have started doing drugs, much less dealing them.

"Actually, Lydia is the main reason I'm here today," Terri said.

Tanner's stomach turned to lead and he thought he might be physically sick. He took a series of quick breaths to get oxygen flowing into his system. What had his sister done now? And how much worse was this going to get?

"What about Lydia?" he asked through a tense jaw. "Has she…done something to get into more trouble?"

Terri's gaze widened in surprise. "Oh, no, it's nothing like that. Quite the opposite, actually. Lydia has been a model prisoner. She's even completed an accelerated associate's degree while behind bars."

"A college degree?" Tanner repeated, stunned.

Terri smiled and nodded. "In business administration. She really applied herself. You should be very proud of her."

"I—I am," Tanner stammered. "Stunned. But proud."

His sister studying for a degree? He couldn't even begin to imagine her having the patience and persistence needed to crack a book, much less study for a degree. Who would have thought jail might turn out to be the best thing that ever happened to her?

She'd never even mentioned her studies to him during the few times they'd spoken over the phone during the previous months. Lydia always kept the calls short and sweet—wanting to know how Mackenzie was doing, but only in general terms. If he started to tell her a story about what Mackenzie had done that day, Lydia would immediately cut him off and end the call. And she never talked about herself.

He supposed he understood. It was just too hard for her.

"Lydia is coming up in front of the parole board next Monday," Terri informed them.

"What?" Again, Tanner was stunned. Why hadn't Lydia called and told him what was going on? "I hadn't heard."

"No," Terri said. "Lydia said she hadn't spoken with you. I guess she thought it would be easier coming from me."

"She'll be out of jail, then?" Rebecca asked. She met Tanner's gaze across the table and gave him a slight nod. "She can, of course, come live here at the ranch until she can find a job and a place of her own."

Tanner's shoulders tensed so tightly he couldn't turn his neck. As kind as it was for Rebecca to make such an offer, he really didn't want his sister living here.

That probably made him the worst brother ever, but so be it. He had his hands and heart full of responsibilities as it was.

Lydia living at the ranch would cause added stress on Rebecca that she just didn't need right now, especially not as close as she was to giving birth to their son. Tanner refused to put her in that position, even if her kind heart instinctively reached out to those in need—maybe especially because it did.

And having Lydia around Mackenzie would be nothing short of a complete disaster, unless she really had changed as much as Terri seemed to think she had.

That remained to be seen. There must be some better way to do this.

But Rebecca had put them in a real bind by speaking up as she had. How was he going to delicately rescind the offer without coming off as the biggest jerk and worst brother in the world?

Thankfully, Terri spoke first.

"I'm sure Lydia would appreciate the offer," said Terri. "But that won't be necessary. If the parole board agrees to her release, she'll be mandated to a monitored halfway house. She'll live with several other women who are trying to get their lives together after jail. It's a new program Texas is trying. She'll have houseparents and will have strict rules as to what she can and can't do and where she can and can't go. She'll be responsible to get and keep a job—with help, of course. We have specific placement for these women, businesses that know what we are about and are willing to give these ladies a second chance. But it's a very strict environment. If they come back to the house drunk or high even once, they will return to jail. This is their second chance. They won't get a third."

That, Tanner thought, might be where Lydia would fail. Would she have the willpower to stay away from drugs?

Then again, it sounded like she'd made a lot of changes while she was in jail. Maybe—hopefully—she was a new woman. Perhaps even someone who could take back her parenting rights and give Mackenzie the mother's love she so desperately needed.

Oh, how he wanted to believe that. He prayed every day for Lydia.

But Tanner knew his sister better than anyone. And sad to say, he wasn't holding his breath.

"What will happen with Mackenzie?" Tanner asked. He was ashamed at the relief he felt that he wouldn't be directly responsible for his sister. He'd been responsible for her ever since they were both kids. Now he had a family of his own to worry about.

"Mackenzie is the other reason I'm here. We would like you to continue being her full-time guardian until such time as your sister is released into the general public."

"No question," Tanner assured her. "As I said earlier, Mackenzie is family."

"Excellent." Terri wrote something in her notes that Tanner couldn't quite make out.

"There is one other thing," Terri continued. "Lydia may be granted supervised visitation rights, if everything goes well."

Tanner's heart warmed. He knew how much his sister longed to see Mackenzie, even if they never talked about it.

"What is that going to look like?" Rebecca asked. "Will we be taking Mackenzie to see Lydia, or the other way around? Will we be in charge of supervising the visits?"

"Oh, no, that's the social worker's responsibility— namely, me. I will pick up Lydia from the halfway house and bring her here to the ranch, if that's okay with you. Either you or Tanner, or both of you, are welcome to remain in the room with Mackenzie and Lydia as they interact. If you could provide a box of toys for them to play with, that will make it easier on Lydia, who will no doubt feel awkward and uncomfortable at first. Having toys which are familiar to Mackenzie will in turn help Mackenzie feel more at ease with her mother."

"We'll do everything we can to make this success-ful," Rebecca assured her.

Terri beamed at Rebecca. "I know you will. I have a good feeling about the two of you. If anyone can help Lydia in this situation, it's you two."

She stood and gathered her things and Tanner walked her to the door.

"I'll be in touch as soon as the parole board has made their decision," Terri said.

"We'll be waiting," Tanner replied, his gut as hard as a rock.

He knew he was being selfish, but why did this have to happen now, when there was already so much stress in their lives?

Just once, couldn't they catch a break?

* * *

"Talk to me." Rebecca folded her hands on the table and caught Tanner's eye. He was visibly upset, from his trembling hands to the pulse beating at the corner of his tight jaw. "What are you thinking right now?"

He groaned and slumped back in his chair. "You don't want to know."

"Surprise me."

He scoffed. "You'll be surprised, all right—or maybe not so much. I have to be the most self-centered, callous man on this planet."

She smiled softly. "Well, I know *that's* not true."

And she did. Amnesia or no amnesia, she knew the kind of man Tanner Hamilton was, and he wasn't selfish or callous. He was the sweetest, most generous man she'd ever known, although she was fairly certain her tough, rugged cowboy would balk if she said those words out loud, so she swallowed them back.

He gave everything for his family. When the necessity arose, he'd become Mackenzie's guardian without blinking an eye—something Rebecca doubted most men in his position would have done. He'd taken Rebecca in—even to the point of letting her live on the ranch with him—when she'd needed him the most, even though she'd been the one to leave him. He had to have been carrying anger and resentment for her, and yet he hadn't let his own feelings get in the way of doing what was right.

"So tell me what's bothering you," she urged. "Maybe I can help."

He reached across the table and took her hand. "You

already help, just by being here. More than you know. Your presence gives me courage. It's just—I'm not sure Lydia is going to be ready for the outside world."

"Isn't that for the parole board to decide?"

He nodded. "But the parole board doesn't know Lydia like I do. She might have put on an act for them in jail, but I'm afraid the first thing she'll do when she gets out is find a way to score some heroin. She's brilliant when it comes to finding drugs. She may have detoxed in jail, but I'm still not convinced that won't be the first thing on her mind. Is that an awful thing for a brother to say?" He was clearly racked with guilt, and Rebecca wished she knew a way to take some of the burden off his shoulders.

"Terri made it sound like she's really turned her life around, taking advantage of everything jail had to offer. She got a college degree. Maybe she really has learned from her mistakes."

"Maybe." Tanner ran a hand across his stubbled jaw. "This is going to sound terrible, but I was relieved when Lydia got arrested and went to jail. It was hard on Mackenzie, of course, but not as hard as it would have been to grow up with a mother whose only concern was when and where she was going to get her next fix. Trust me. I should know."

"I'm so sorry," Rebecca said, squeezing his hand, and he realized she wouldn't remember what she'd once known about his past. She would have no idea that Tanner and Lydia had grown up with a mother who was an addict.

"Lydia and I are actually half brother and sister. My

mom was never very responsible with her life. I don't know who my father is. She never made any attempt to find him. Then Lydia came along three years later. Same song, different verse. Mom rarely spent more than a week or two with any man. Looking back on it, I'm guessing her relationships had more to do with finding her next hit than being in any kind of romance.

"I learned at a very young age that Mom wasn't fit to raise us. I learned a lot of other things sooner than I should have, as well—like how to use my mom's food stamp card to buy real groceries and not just junk food. She couldn't buy drugs with the card so it didn't mean much to her. Thankfully, Mom didn't care enough to do the shopping herself, so I was able to put food on the table, even when I was in late elementary school. The grocer down the street from us where I shopped knew of our circumstances and looked the other way when I bought food with the card. I'm pretty sure he wasn't supposed to do that, but he literally saved our lives with his kindness."

"I can't even imagine," Rebecca said, releasing a long, heavy breath. The truth was, she *was* imagining the scene in great detail, and it was breaking her heart. A young boy trying to take care of his little sister while his mother sat in the living room watching TV, high as a kite. A kid pushing a grocery cart that was bigger than he was, trying to decide what food would be the most healthy and nutritious for him and his sister and that wouldn't be too hard for him to cook.

"I went door to door at neighboring ranches asking

to do chores for money. It never seemed to be enough, but at least social services never got involved."

Rebecca was stunned. It was no wonder he didn't trust Lydia with Mackenzie. Not after all he'd been through.

"We'll make it work, Tanner. No matter what happens with Lydia. We will protect Mackenzie. I just want you to know I'll be right there by your side, keeping Mackenzie safe. That will be our first priority."

Tanner's eyes lit up with gratitude he couldn't express with words.

"Now, if you'll excuse me, I am going to go write down all the things we just discussed so I'll have a clear head and all the pertinent details when Lydia comes to visit Mackenzie."

Writing notes to herself had become second nature to her. But notes could only go so far—they couldn't arrest the emotions that went along with each situation. They couldn't capture a snapshot of Tanner's stress and why this was so difficult for him.

She slipped her cell phone into the back pocket of her jeans. It was the best she could do. She would have to take the emotions as they came, day-to-day.

And maybe—just maybe—she would start to remember.

Chapter Ten

Tanner urged his gray quarter horse gelding Gusto to the left of the herd of cows in order to drive them to the right and into another pasture where they would find fresh grazing ground. Herding cattle out on the grassy plain was one of his favorite jobs as a rancher. It connected him to the past and the many, many ranchers who'd herded cattle in just this same way over centuries of time.

The wind in his face, the muddled sounds of confused cows as they tried to figure out what they were supposed to do, the squeals of the newborn calves who didn't want to be separated from their mothers—this was the life he'd always wanted, and he loved every second of it, even during the hard times.

Once he'd gotten the herd through to the next field, he slid off Gusto's back and closed the gate behind them. He had a lot to do. With everything that had been going on at home, it had been a couple of weeks since he'd ridden the fence line and checked for breaks.

But he'd have to do that later. Right now, he needed to get back to the ranch house and get cleaned up.

Lydia's parole had been granted last week and she'd moved into the halfway house. Today, Terri was bringing her by for her first supervised visit with Mackenzie. Tanner's chest was in knots just thinking about it. He hadn't seen Lydia since the day she'd been incarcerated—her choice, not his. She hadn't wanted anyone to see her that way, not even her brother—and especially not Mackenzie.

If he'd had his way, he would have visited her in jail at least once every week, despite the fact that he would have lost a day's work every time. And during some of those visits he would have brought Mackenzie, so she could interact with her mama.

But Lydia had been humiliated by her arrest and subsequent incarceration and insisted that no one visit her at all.

He guessed he understood why she thought the way she did, although he couldn't imagine being away from his child for any length of time. Mackenzie was so precious, and Lydia had missed so much.

Then again, he couldn't imagine spending time in jail. He and Lydia had grown up in the same household, in the same atmosphere, and he was well aware how it could have been him behind bars. But God had rescued him from following in his mother's footsteps and had set him on a straight path, for which he would be eternally grateful. Instead of hanging out with the bad crowd in high school, someone had invited him to youth group at church, and there he'd found new friends and a way of life much different than the one he experienced at home. He'd tried over and over to get Lydia to accompany him to church, but she'd refused.

He hoped and prayed Lydia had found something similar in jail, someone who would lead her to a Savior who loved her unconditionally. Tanner knew of at least three separate jail ministries that worked there and he'd spoken with the directors of all of them. Every night in his prayers, Tanner begged God to intercede on Lydia's behalf and reach out to her in His great mercy.

Soon enough, he would know whether or not his prayers had been answered.

When he arrived back at the ranch house, he found everyone in the kitchen with a simple lunch of cold cuts, cheese and bread on the table, along with all the fixins for a Dagwood sandwich, Tanner's absolute favorite. He loved to create an artful pile of meat, cheese, mustard, mayo, pickles, lettuce and tomatoes between slices of bread until he had a sandwich so high he had to smash it with his palm before it would fit in his mouth. He even added a layer of cheese balls to give it a little more crunch.

But before he could eat, he excused himself to shower and put on fresh clothes. When he returned, everyone had their sandwiches on their plates in front of them. To his surprise, Tanner's Dagwood sandwich had been made and was ready to go on a plate before his seat at the head of the table.

"Who did this?" he asked, checking the layers to make sure nothing had been missed. He didn't think he'd ever seen a nicer-looking Dagwood sandwich in his life, because someone in this household had made it for him—in love.

Rebecca waved her hand, her cheeks coloring prettily. "I did. I hope I made it right. I watched you the last time you made one for yourself and wrote myself a note to keep it all straight. That's one serious sandwich."

"I do take my Dagwoods seriously," he agreed. "And this one looks perfect. Thank you."

"Whew." Rebecca wiped fake sweat from her brow. "I can breathe now. I feel like I passed the wife test."

He raised a brow, his pulse kicking up when the word *wife* came out of Rebecca's mouth. He would never get used to hearing that. It felt new all over again, like when they were first married. Only this time, he wasn't going to take it for granted.

Not ever.

"Wife test?" he echoed, each word tasting increasingly delicious on his tongue, more than any sandwich could ever be.

"Yeah, you know. Understanding what makes my husband tick. The way to a man's heart is through his stomach. Don't ask me how I know that."

He took a bite of his sandwich and groaned in delight. "Well, you got this right."

Rebecca beamed.

The table was a little quieter than usual as they ate, without as much casual chatter as usually went on during their meals. Everyone was nervous about the afternoon to come, and clearly Mackenzie was picking up on that, because she just sat quietly and picked at her food.

They'd decided not to tell her what was happening

until after lunch, when Rebecca took her to her room to wash her hands and face and put a pretty pink bow in her hair.

Tanner and Peggy were waiting in the living room when Rebecca made a big announcement that Princess Mackenzie was on her way. Tanner couldn't help but grin when Rebecca rolled up her hand and tooted her pretend trumpet as Mackenzie entered and spun around, showing off both her bright pink skirt and the matching bow in her hair.

"Wow," Tanner enthused. "Be still my heart. What beautiful girls I have living in my house. I'm the most blessed man ever." His smile was ostensibly for Mackenzie, but he slyly winked at Rebecca.

He was fairly certain she blushed, and his heart rate kicked up a notch.

"Why are we all dressed up?" Mackenzie asked, studying the adults around her. "Is it church day already?"

Tanner chuckled.

Rebecca knelt by Mackenzie. "No, it's not church day, Mackenzie, but it is a very special day. In a few minutes, your mama will be here to visit with you."

Mackenzie's eyes widened. "Mama?"

"That's right," Tanner said, wondering just how much the little girl would remember about what had happened with her mama. He remembered those first awful nights when Mackenzie would cry herself to sleep. He didn't know what the little girl comprehended about suddenly being sent to live with her uncle Tanner, but judging by the light in her eyes, she understood what was about to happen now—at least enough to fill her with joy.

"Your mama can't wait to see you, and hug you, and talk with you and play with you," Rebecca added.

"Mama," Mackenzie exclaimed, giggling and clapping her pudgy hands.

So far, so good.

Tanner pulled in a deep breath and let it out slowly. All systems were go. Now they just had to wait for Terri to arrive with Lydia and pray that his sister would be able to deal with the awkwardness of this situation. He certainly was feeling it. Nothing about this day was normal.

He glanced at his fitness watch. Five minutes to go until blastoff.

He only hoped the rocket would soar into space and not immediately do a U-turn and crash back to earth, or worse yet, go up in flames.

Peggy parked herself on the rocking chair and took up her knitting with the alpaca wool they'd recently sheared. Rebecca pulled out the princess dollhouse that was in the corner among other toys they planned to use to help Lydia interact with Mackenzie. Soon, Rebecca and Mackenzie were lost in the world of beautiful princesses, charming princes and hopefully, a happily-ever-after—if those even existed anymore.

Tanner paced the living room, glancing out the front window as he went, watching for the telltale cloud of dust that would indicate someone was coming up their long, unpaved drive. As he stalked back and forth, he forced himself to breathe and keep his face neutral of emotion, even though there'd been few times in his life when he was as anxious as he was at this moment.

Where *were* they?

He didn't know that much about Terri, but from the professional way she dressed and how organized she'd always appeared, he just assumed she was one of those people who were always on time.

Maybe not. It wasn't quite time to panic.

Yet.

But when another forty-five minutes had gone by and still no Terri and Lydia, Tanner was ready to jump out of his skin.

"I'll put Mackenzie down for her nap," offered Peggy. Tanner was glad for a moment alone to speak with Rebecca and suspected that was part of the reason Peggy had offered, God bless her.

"Where are they?" he asked through gritted teeth as he stared out the front window. He clenched his fists, barely resisting the urge to punch the air. "There's something seriously wrong here. I can feel it."

He nearly jumped when Rebecca slid her arms around his waist from behind him and laid her head against his back. "I don't know," she whispered. "I wish I could assure you everything is fine, but I don't think it is. There is no reason I can think of why Terri would just not show up without calling or anything to let us know she'd be late."

"Exactly."

Suddenly, Tanner's cell phone buzzed in his pocket, startling him. He pulled it out so quickly he nearly dropped it before looking at the screen.

"It's Terri," he said as he turned in Rebecca's arms.

His gaze met her worried one, but she nodded in encouragement.

He took a deep breath and let it out before answering.

"Terri, where are you?" he asked in lieu of a greeting. "We've been waiting nearly an hour and had to put Mackenzie down for a nap."

"I'm afraid it's not good news," Terri said. Tanner frowned and grabbed Rebecca's hand, leading them both to the couch. He had a feeling he was going to need to be sitting down to hear what Terri was about to say.

"Your sister has disappeared."

"She's *what*?" he growled, not knowing whether to be angry or afraid. "What do you mean she's disappeared? I thought she was under strict supervision?"

"She is. She went to the restroom at the restaurant where she's busing tables and slipped out through the window. As of yet, we haven't been able to find her."

Tanner pinched the bridge of his nose and blew out a frustrated breath. "Where have you looked?"

"She's not anywhere she is allowed to be. She knows the rules. She walks straight from the halfway house to the nearby restaurant, performs her shift and returns home. She's not allowed to make any other stops or go anywhere but work and home. Her houseparents haven't seen her since this morning when she left for work. The police are looking for her now."

"Tell them to look where she's likely to score drugs," he said tightly.

"Tanner," Rebecca said raggedly, clutching his arm.

He glared down at her, even though it wasn't Rebecca's fault any of this was happening. He hoped she realized his expression wasn't directed at her. "Look. I'm just telling it like it is. You want to find her? That's where to look."

When Rebecca's beautiful copper-penny eyes filled with tears, he felt like the worst human being on earth.

"You can be assured we'll find her soon," Terri said. Tanner was so broken up over the news he had almost forgotten she was on the other end of the line.

"Call me when you have her," he said briskly.

"Look. Let's not jump to any conclusions," Terri said, although Tanner could hear the doubt in her voice. "It may be nothing."

"You think that if it makes you feel better."

Rebecca reached for his phone and gently took it away from him, massaging her free hand over his neck.

"Thank you for letting us know what's going on, Terri," she said. "Is there anything else we can do? Shall we take a car and go looking ourselves? Oh, I see. Yes, I understand. I'll let him know."

Rebecca ended the call with an audible sigh. She pushed the hair off her forehead, only to have it drop down again, brushing her high cheekbones.

Her tell. She was as anxious and frustrated as he was.

"What? What did she say?" he pressed.

"That it's very important for you and me to remain where we are in case Lydia decides to show up here at the ranch."

Tanner snorted. "What are the chances of that? Lydia is many things, but she's not stupid. She understood what was supposed to happen today, and she made her choice. If she were going to come to the ranch and visit

with Mackenzie, she would have done so with Terri."
His stomach churned until he thought he might be sick.
"I could be of far more use driving around San Antonio looking for her. I know some of her old haunts. I
can't just sit here and do nothing, no matter what the
police say."

Rebecca took both of his hands in hers. "We won't
be doing nothing," she assured him. "We'll be praying for Lydia."

It had been the longest two hours of Rebecca's life,
not only worrying about where Lydia was and what she
might be doing, but trying to keep Tanner from wearing
a hole in the carpet. He was like a caged tiger, ready to
pounce on anything that moved.

She wished there were something she could do to
help—Tanner, Lydia, Terri, the police—anybody, at
this point—but the resolution was entirely out of her
hands. Until they found Lydia and definitively determined what had happened, Tanner would remain in his
agitated state, and even then, it was hard to tell if he was
going to go off like fireworks or if all the air would go
out of him and he would completely deflate.

He was well-muscled from ranch work, and for hours
now, every sinew in his shoulders and biceps had been
tight with strain. His eyebrows were drawn in a permanent scowl and he occasionally muttered something
under his breath from between gritted teeth.

Rebecca had checked on Mackenzie a couple of
times. Peggy had fallen asleep beside the little girl,
and the two of them looked incredibly peaceful lying

there in Mackenzie's little twin bed with Mackenzie's head lightly resting on Peggy's chest, which moved up and down slowly and evenly in the tranquility of sleep.

Rebecca took a moment just to breathe. She didn't know when or how this would end, but no matter what, she would be there to support her husband and the little girl who meant so much to him.

When the news finally came, it wasn't good.

The police had picked up Lydia. She wasn't buying drugs, but selling them, out on the street, as flagrantly and carelessly as she'd apparently always done. She didn't even try to run away when the uniformed officers approached her.

That fact gave Rebecca reason to question. It was almost as if Lydia *wanted* to be arrested.

But there was no question about what would happen now.

She hadn't learned a single thing in her time in jail. It was unthinkable to Rebecca that Lydia would choose selling drugs over seeing her baby girl, especially after being away from her so long. She'd had a chance to make things right today, but instead had chosen to follow the wrong path yet again.

Now she had nothing to look forward to but returning to the jail from which she'd just been released. Rebecca suspected that, like last time, Lydia would not accept support from her brother, which would break Tanner's heart anew.

Lydia had made her own choices, whereas Mackenzie could not. But even though it would be hard to grow up without her biological mother, that little girl had Tanner, and he would never let her down. And she had Peggy, too.

At that moment, in spite of not knowing what her memories might contain, Rebecca made a heartfelt commitment to Mackenzie, as well. As a family, they would do everything they could to give Mackenzie the best life could offer.

Rebecca waited silently until Tanner hung up the phone and slid it back into his pocket. Though he stood with his back toward her, facing the front window, where now he knew no one would be coming down the drive, she'd managed to understand most of the conversation. She waited for him to speak, to tell her what he was thinking, since she couldn't see his expression.

No doubt he was angry at being betrayed once again by a person close to him, one of the few people he'd let into his heart, someone for whom he'd sacrificed and given all his love—something Rebecca now knew didn't come easy for him.

Suddenly, she realized his shoulders were shaking, and her ears picked up the softest and most heartbreaking sound she'd ever heard in her life.

A grown man weeping.

"Tanner?" she whispered, reaching out to him and grasping his biceps.

He turned and wrapped his arms around her, burying his face in her hair as he silently sobbed. She gripped him as tightly to her as she could, their unborn baby tucked between them. She didn't say a word, but simply allowed him to release his emotions for as long as he needed her. She was his literal shoulder to cry on, and there was nowhere on earth she'd rather be.

After a minute or two, he stiffened and pulled back, pressing his palms over his eyelids to wipe away all traces of tears. He then jammed his hands into the front pockets of his jeans and turned away from her once again, clearly struggling to lock down his feelings.

She rubbed a palm over his back. He might want to pull away from her and bury his emotions, but she wasn't going to let him.

Not this time.

Where had that thought come from?

It stunned her with as much electricity as a lightning bolt would have done.

It must have come from somewhere, but what did it mean? Was something from her past trying to edge out and jolt her current reality?

No. This couldn't be happening. She'd been desperately trying to discover her past during the last few weeks, but this wasn't the time for her amnesia to disappear. There was only so much she could deal with at once.

With effort, she pushed those thoughts aside to dwell on later. Right now, Tanner needed her.

"Talk to me," she whispered, her voice cracking as tears slid down her cheeks.

"I just… I hoped… I *prayed* that I'd be wrong this time."

"I know."

"How could she do this to Mackenzie?"

"Mackenzie's not the only one Lydia has hurt today,"

Rebecca pointed out, wanting Tanner to talk about his own feelings. Yes, the most urgent and pressing matter was how they were going to deal with Mackenzie, but Rebecca didn't think what was going to happen to the little girl was the only reason Tanner was having a breakdown. For a moment, when he'd first turned around and embraced her, she'd glimpsed in his eyes the little boy who'd had to give up his own life to take care of his little sister.

Now she saw a man ready to give up his own life to take care of his little sister's child.

Tanner ignored Rebecca's prompt.

"What are we going to tell her?" he asked, his voice ragged. "We promised her that she'd see her mama today. Now it's very likely that she won't see her mama for years, maybe not until she's an adult herself. I doubt Lydia is going to be any more open to jail visits from me and her daughter than she was before. It makes me sick that she's abandoned her own child in this way."

"Poor Mackenzie. I shouldn't have said anything to her about her mama coming around," Rebecca said, thinking back to what she'd told the preschooler. "You tried to warn me there was a possibility Lydia wouldn't follow through with the supervised visitation. I should have listened to you and waited until she was here before I mentioned anything."

Tanner tucked her under his shoulder and brushed a kiss against her hair. "You couldn't have known things would play out the way they did."

"But *you* knew."

He shook his head and was about to say more when

Peggy entered the room carrying a wide-eyed Mackenzie on her hip.

"Any news?" she asked, plopping Mackenzie down in the corner next to her toys.

"They found Lydia," Rebecca said softly.

"I didn't know they lost her. What happened?"

"Long story short," said Tanner, "she snuck out of the restaurant where she was supposed to be working and headed straight back to her old friends—and her old life. The police caught her selling drugs."

"Oh my," Peggy breathed. "What's going to happen now?" She glanced toward Mackenzie.

Tanner set his jaw. "I'm going to seek permanent guardianship. I want to adopt her as soon as the courts will allow."

She knew he was really shaken up, but there were two things about Tanner's statement that bothered Rebecca.

First, he'd said *I*, not *we*. Second, he didn't look at her when he said it.

Her heart clenched and she laid a protective hand over her belly.

Did he not see her as a permanent part of this picture? She was his wife. This was their family. She couldn't let that shake her. Not on something this important.

"I agree," Rebecca said, verbally throwing her hat into the ring. "We should make this arrangement with Mackenzie permanent."

"I'm her only living relative, so it should be pretty straightforward. I'm the most logical person to take over her guardianship."

Peggy raised her brow and looked from Tanner to Rebecca, who shrugged miserably. But now wasn't the time to bring this up with Tanner. It was a discussion they needed to have sooner rather than later, but first they needed to break the news to Mackenzie that her mama wasn't coming for a visit.

She reached out and took Tanner's hand, offering her support even though he hadn't asked for it.

He blew out a breath, combed his fingers back through his hair and led Rebecca to the corner where Mackenzie was playing.

He crouched to the three-year-old's level. "What would you say to a hot-fudge sundae at Cup O' Jo's Café?"

"Yes, please," the little girl answered with a big smile. "Are we going to bring my mama with us?"

Tanner's panicked gaze met Rebecca's.

"I'm afraid not, sweetheart," Rebecca said tentatively. "She wanted us to tell you that she loves you lots and she's sorry she couldn't make it to visit you today."

"Oh." The smile left the child's lips, but only for a moment. "Can I have strawberry ice cream instead?"

All three adults let out a sigh of relief. If only they could pivot their emotions as easily as children did.

"Strawberry it is, then," Tanner promised. "You can even get two big scoops if you want."

"With a cherry on top," Rebecca promised. "If you like cherries, that is."

"Yummy," Mackenzie assured her, and then turned serious. "What's your favorite flavor, Auntie Rebecca?"

Her eyes widened. What *was* her favorite flavor of ice cream? She didn't have a clue.

"Mint chocolate chip smothered in chocolate sauce," Tanner answered for her.

That did sound good—or at least, good enough to try.

"Can I get that at Cup O' Jo's?" she asked.

"Absolutely. They have the best ice cream ever."

Rebecca's stomach rumbled. "I think I'm having a pregnancy craving."

Not that she really knew what a pregnancy craving felt like. She was just hungry all the time.

"Well, then, girls, we'd best get you all to Cup O' Jo's, pronto."

Rebecca watched Mackenzie closely, but the little girl really did seem okay with not seeing her mother today. Rebecca thanked God she hadn't said more about the visit when she'd mentioned Lydia to Mackenzie in the first place. How much worse could she have made it?

But now they needed to look forward—to pulling together as a family and adopting precious Mackenzie.

She glanced at Tanner, who was still a tense wall of tight muscles. She suspected it would take him a good deal longer to process what was happening than it had with Mackenzie.

Was he blaming himself?

Why would he? None of this was his fault. And yet ultimately, just as it had been when he was a young boy caring for his sister, the responsibility to make all things right fell upon him. He would blame himself for Lydia's crimes. Maybe he didn't realize it, but Lydia returning to jail might just be the best thing that could have happened to Mackenzie. She was going to grow up in a happy family. Tanner would love her and protect her, something her own mother could never do.

Not only that, but Tanner wasn't alone this time. Rebecca was here now, and no matter what her memories did or did not eventually reveal, she and Tanner were building a *new* relationship together, one she vowed she would not leave.

Chapter Eleven

All the next week, Tanner brooded about what to do with his family. His emotions were all over the place. He was angry and frustrated about Lydia, who was already back in jail—but that was her problem. She'd made her choices, and he just had to let that go.

Was it wrong that, in a way, he was happy Mackenzie got to stay with them? During the time the little girl had been part of their family, he had grown to love her as much as if she were his own daughter and not just his niece. Rebecca had indicated she felt the same way and was helping him do the necessary due diligence to find out how to permanently adopt Mackenzie into their family.

He knew he stood a much better chance of an adoption successfully going through with Rebecca by his side. While Tanner was Mackenzie's only other blood relative, being able to offer her a home with both male and female role models would be a huge boon to him.

So it was all going as well as it might, and that was what worried Tanner most of all.

He'd been seeing little things with Rebecca—stuff he wasn't sure she even consciously thought about but that were singular to her. The way she loaded the dishwasher, for example. Plates went in one direction by size, silverware facing downward—spoons first, forks second and knives at the back, where Mackenzie couldn't reach them should she accidentally get into the dishwasher. The way Rebecca folded laundry. It was a chore he enjoyed doing with her—something they'd done at the beginning of their marriage but had lost as the years went on and Tanner had gotten more focused on the ranch. He would fold a T-shirt and put it on the pile, only to have Rebecca take it off again and fold it *correctly*. That was exactly what she used to do, back when they were first married, only he was fairly sure she didn't even know it.

He was definitely falling back in love with his wife and for the first time in years, was looking forward to their future together—him, Rebecca and their growing family. But what would happen when she regained her memory?

This could all be gone in a flash, and he wasn't sure he could survive another heartbreak like the one he'd suffered before. And this one would be a million times worse, now that Mackenzie and their unborn son figured into the picture.

The day Lydia hadn't shown up to visit with Mackenzie, he had spoken of taking responsibility for her—him alone. He'd seen the hurt in Rebecca's eyes and knew it was because he hadn't included her in his declaration.

But how could he? She would never forgive him for all the mistakes he'd made in their marriage, if only she knew. He couldn't ask her to stay around for the children's sake. It wasn't fair to ask her to make that kind of sacrifice. And he wasn't sure he could live with her knowing she couldn't stand to be in the same room with him.

No. He wanted a real marriage in every way, love, respect and support weaving through every aspect of both of their lives.

There was no good answer.

He was grateful to have Rebecca here now. After the day Lydia had ditched them, Mackenzie had gone back to having nightmares and crying out in the night, suffering just as she'd done when her mother had first gone away.

This time, though, Rebecca was there with her. Mackenzie responded to her sweet, female voice as Rebecca sang gentle lullabies and assured the child all was well. Rebecca was such a natural with the preschooler, and she was going to be an equally amazing mother to their son.

Tanner had come up with an idea that he thought might help Mackenzie through the worst of her nightmares and provide her with a special kind of companionship so she wouldn't be alone in the night. Likewise, his son would be blessed. And it would also go a long way into putting himself into Rebecca's good graces— or at least, he hoped it would.

There was a time when his surprise would have gone well, beyond a doubt, and he wouldn't be feeling as worried as he was right now.

But now he wasn't so sure about his actions. He prayed some things hadn't changed—but the truth was, he wasn't sure of anything anymore. For better or for worse, he couldn't go on until he came clean about everything.

He just couldn't continue to go on without a clean slate. He wasn't exactly lying, but by allowing her amnesia to wipe out the bad parts of their marriage, he might as well be. A real marriage was the mixture of the ups and the downs, the highs and lows, the sadness along with the joy. The fights—and making up again. Not about letting the sun go down on their anger—and then allowing months to go by with no sun at all in their relationship.

It was time to tell Rebecca the truth—the whole truth.

He'd speak with Peggy and see if she couldn't watch Mackenzie one day this week, and he would take Rebecca someplace special—their own private spot on the river where he had proposed, and where she had allowed him to slide the diamond solitaire—one she no longer wore—on her finger. He didn't even know what she'd done with her wedding ring—only that when she'd first arrived back in Serendipity, she hadn't been wearing it.

He pulled his truck into his neighbor Nick McKenna's driveway and shut off the engine. Like Tanner, Nick was a rancher, with a family spread twice the size of Tanner's and double the head of cattle.

What Tanner *didn't* have was a dog. And what Nick

did have, at the moment, was a whole litter of them. Tanner had pulled Nick aside the previous Sunday and inquired about getting one of the puppies for his niece.

Rebecca had grown up with dogs and after the miscarriage, she had begged Tanner to let her get one, but he'd always held off. He didn't even know why, really. He liked dogs as much as the next man. It had just never seemed like the right time. It wasn't as if he didn't have enough responsibilities already, and Rebecca hadn't been in any kind of condition to take care of a puppy.

Now, though, he thought a puppy might be just the thing to brighten everyone's day. And getting a sheltie made good business sense to him, as well.

Nick met him at the truck and shook his hand.

"Ready to go see the pups?" he asked. "I'm warning you now, they're a real handful. Loud and wiggly."

That was kind of the point, and Tanner grinned at his friend.

Nick led him into his house and back to the den.

"I gotta admit—I spoil my dogs. Most working dogs sleep in the barn, but I've always kept mine inside with me."

Tanner's eyes widened when he saw the five wiggly multicolored, brown-eyed poof balls running around the room or wrestling with each other. Only the puppies' mama appeared calm—or maybe exhausted—lying on her side in her doggie bed. With all the din in the room from barking puppies, Tanner could hardly make out Nick's voice when he spoke.

"Are you looking for a male or female?" Nick asked.

"I've got two males and three females, although I think one of the males has been spoken for."

"I don't know," Tanner admitted, feeling slightly overwhelmed. He hadn't actually gotten past the idea of getting a puppy. He had no idea how to choose one. "I'm embarrassed to admit I never really thought about it. This is sort of an impulse purchase for my wife and my niece."

Nick grinned. "Trust me. There's no better way to a woman's heart than with a puppy."

"Yeah, that's what I'm hoping. I need to win over a couple of hearts in that house."

If anyone would know about winning female hearts, it would be Nick McKenna. He'd dated almost every single girl in Serendipity at one time or another, and had now moved on to a pretty blonde who was new in town.

"Feel free to look them over and interact with them. You can take as much time as you want."

Tanner vaguely waved his hand toward the puppies. "How do I choose which one will be best for Rebecca and Mackenzie? Or does it matter?"

"Take a seat," Nick said, gesturing toward an old couch.

Immediately, the puppies came to investigate him, and soon he had five wiggly bodies all around him. This was more confusing than just watching them play on the floor, and Tanner barely kept himself from pointing out that this was going to make the choice harder, not easier. He couldn't even tell one puppy from another.

"You look a little overwhelmed," Nick remarked, punctuating his sentence with a laugh.

"You think?"

"It's been my experience that if you're patient, a puppy will choose you. Just let them have a little time with you and see what happens."

"Okay." Tanner slid off the couch and knelt on the floor, letting the puppies come to him and trying his best to tell one from the other. He watched for differences in their colored coats and the crazy characteristics that went along with each pup.

After a few minutes, he was starting to be able to distinguish one puppy from another. The two male pups were the wrestlers. They'd come up and sniff him from time to time, but then would immediately go back to their game, rolling over each other, oblivious that he was still sitting there.

The three females showed considerably more interest in their guest. All three were pretty, with fluffy multicolored, blue-merle coats he knew would delight Rebecca and Mackenzie. Any one of the three would work, he decided as he picked up one and set her on his lap, running his hand over her soft coat for a moment. This one had character, bumping his palm to be petted and then plopping right down in his lap and rolling over for a tummy scratch. Tanner chuckled and willingly obliged.

After a moment, Tanner set her down and scooped up the next.

But as he placed the second one back on the floor and started to reach for the third, the first little puppy crawled back onto his lap, nosing her way in, and she stubbornly refused to give up her spot on Tanner's lap to puppy number three.

Nick laughed. "See? What did I tell you?"

"Huh. What do you know?"

As a test, he put the pup who'd *chosen* him back on the floor, facing away from him, and gave her rump a little boost. She turned right around and barked at him, chewing him out but good for abandoning her, and then leaped straight back into his arms.

"I guess that's it, then. Do you have a collar and lead for her?" Nick asked.

Tanner shook his head. "Like I said, I didn't think this through very well, other than just having the vague idea that a puppy might brighten everyone's spirits."

"Not a problem. I'll loan you what you need and you can visit Emerson's when you have the opportunity. You know how the ladies are with shopping. They'll probably appreciate the excuse to go out and buy all new things for their new puppy."

Tanner chuckled. His real problem was he didn't know the ladies—everyone from his mother-in-law, to his wife, and right down to his three-year-old niece. They were all a complete mystery to him.

Suddenly he was happy to be having a son. Maybe that would even things out a little bit. He suspected he might have a better idea what to do with a boy. He'd never felt quite comfortable playing dollies and princesses with Mackenzie. But he could teach his son how to throw a football. And invite Mackenzie out to play, as well.

Or maybe he was just hopeless. This fatherhood thing was *huge*.

"What's Mackenzie's favorite color?" Nick asked, digging around through a box marked Dog Stuff.

"I—er—purple, I think."

Nick fastened a purple collar and lead to the Hamiltons' new puppy and scooped puppy food into a baggie. "This will get you by for a day or two. I'll bring her papers on Sunday. You've already got your hands full now."

As best he could with a wiggling puppy in his arms, Tanner pulled his wallet out of the back pocket of his jeans and selected three hundred-dollar bills. "It's three hundred, right?"

Nick shook his head and held up a hand, palm out. "She's on me. I heard in the church prayer time about all of the problems your family is going through right now. I really hope this tiny bundle of energy will give that little girl a reason to smile."

Tanner raised his brows. "You're sure?"

"Absolutely."

Tanner shook Nick's hand. "I really appreciate it, and I know the girls will, too. You're a good friend, Nick."

Nick helped him wrangle the puppy into his truck and before long, Tanner was back home again. He hadn't felt this nervous in a long time, but it was happy nerves, a good kind of excitement. He couldn't wait to introduce Rebecca and Mackenzie to their new puppy.

He honked twice and all three ladies stepped outside on the porch to see what the fuss was about.

He opened the cab door, scooped the puppy into his

arm and carefully set her on the ground. Before he had a chance to grab her lead, the dog had dashed out of his reach—straight toward Mackenzie, wagging her tail wildly and barking an introduction. She definitely knew who she belonged to. Nick had told him dogs were intuitive like that, but Tanner hadn't really believed him until now.

The fluffy ball of fur practically bowled Mackenzie over with her enthusiasm and furiously wagging back end. She jumped and pressed her front paws onto Mackenzie's shoulders, causing the little girl to sit down abruptly. Tanner's heartbeat flared in panic, but then he realized Mackenzie was giggling as the puppy excitedly licked her face.

Rebecca's eyes shone with delight and Tanner grinned at her, walking to her side and slipping his arm around her waist as they enjoyed the Norman Rockwellesque scene of a little girl greeting her puppy for the first time.

"Is it mine, Uncle Tanner?" Mackenzie asked excitedly. Apparently all worn out from the exuberant greeting, the panting puppy flopped down beside the little girl and rested her head on her paws.

"It is a *she*, and yes, Mackenzie, she's your new puppy. You even get to name her and everything."

The child turned suddenly serious, chewing on her bottom lip as she thought. Puppy naming was a serious business, and she didn't want to get it wrong.

"You don't have to decide yet," Tanner told her. "Mr. Nick, the man I got the puppy from, said to watch her personality emerge. Then the right name will just come to you."

He tipped his head down toward Rebecca so his mouth was close to her ear. "And maybe we can help her along a little bit by suggesting good puppy names. Does anything come to mind?" he murmured.

Rebecca shook her head. "No. I think Nick is right. We need to interact with the puppy for a while before we'll be able to pick out the right name."

Tanner shrugged. It didn't make that much of a difference to him one way or the other. He wasn't the type of man to go around naming his animals. If it were left up to him, the poor puppy would probably end up with a moniker like *Dog*.

Rebecca crouched down and ran her hand across the worn-out puppy's thick fur. "She's so soft," she whispered. "I love her coloring. And those big brown eyes! She's perfect."

Tanner chuckled. "Yeah, well, she seems to think so. I didn't pick her out of the litter. She picked me."

"She did what?"

"It was Nick's idea. He said if I just waited long enough, one of the puppies would make it clear that they wanted to go home with me. I didn't believe him, but that was exactly how it happened. Once the pup had claimed me, she wouldn't let any of her littermates near my lap."

She stood and faced him. "That's such a lovely story. God is in everything, even picking out a puppy." Rebecca blinked back tears.

Tanner tensed. Why was she crying? Did she not think getting Mackenzie a puppy was a good thing?

"What's wrong?" he asked, brushing tears off her cheek with the pad of his thumb.

She shook her head and smiled. "Nothing's wrong. These are happy tears. I've always had a soft spot for dogs, ever since I was a child. That, I can remember."

He nodded and swallowed hard. He wouldn't wish amnesia on his worst enemy, but in this case, perhaps her not remembering the whole story was better for them both.

She frowned, her auburn brows forming a V over her nose.

"We didn't have a dog?"

Tanner shrugged.

"*Why* didn't we have a dog? I imagine that would be one of my first orders of business after we tied the knot."

Tanner cleared his throat, which felt like sandpaper.

"It was," he admitted. "You wanted to head out to a rescue facility the moment we got back from our honeymoon."

"Oh. What happened, then? Did we—have one?"

"No. It never seemed to be the right time."

She shook her head. "That makes no sense. Even with my amnesia, you won't be able to convince me of that. There's no wrong time to have a dog, any more than there's a wrong time to have a baby. It's all good. I know some people think if you look at it practically, you have to wait to have a child until later in life when you're more stable. But the truth is you'll never be able to afford to raise a child. And yet babies and dogs are both blessings. I think our household should be full of them."

She *would* think that way. She probably didn't realize it, but she always had. Here she was, a math geek who knew every form of budgeting and accounting, and she threw them all away over dogs and babies. Full house. She trusted God to take care of all of them. Tanner had a harder time with that notion, being a little less able to throw away the practical, although he prayed on a regular basis that the Lord would bless his ever-growing family.

Rebecca laughed and kissed his scraggly cheek. "Thank you. The puppy will be a good playmate for Mackenzie and help keep her mind off—well, you know." She lowered her voice. "I'll bet the puppy will help her with her nightmares, too. Give her the companionship she needs."

"That's the goal," he said, unable to keep from smiling. His throat swelled with emotion.

"Did anyone ever tell you how sweet and thoughtful you are?"

He felt the heat rising to his cheeks.

"You give me too much credit."

"And you don't give yourself enough," she countered.

"Well, as it happens, I didn't just buy the puppy for Mackenzie. She's also for you." He handed her the pup's leash.

"Are you trying to get another kiss?" she teased, then followed through, brushing her lips across his lips this time instead of his cheek.

He'd had no idea the whole puppy idea would go off so well or he would have brought home a dog years ago.

But someone had to be practical, and he hated that it had always been him. Still…

"I didn't buy any stuff for the puppy yet. Nick let me borrow a collar and lead. I thought you and your mom might enjoy taking Mackenzie to Emerson's to get whatever you think the puppy needs. Toys and treats and kibble. In the meantime, Nick has provided us with enough food to get by for a day or two."

"You really are something," she said, running a hand over his jaw.

Hopefully, that was a compliment. There was a time it wouldn't have been.

"Let's take the puppy inside," Rebecca suggested, handing the lead to Mackenzie. I'll find some old blankets and we'll make her a bed. Then we can play with her some more and see what her personality is like. Maybe we'll be able to figure out the right name for her."

Mackenzie gave the puppy a tight hug that the dog immediately wriggled out of.

"Gentle," Rebecca reminded her. Tanner didn't miss the way her hand strayed to her belly.

Puppies and babies. Mackenzie would need to learn how to be gentle with both, because before they knew it, Mackenzie's baby cousin would be arriving.

And Tanner would be a father at last.

Rebecca gasped, but no air entered her lungs. Her eyes were pressed closed but she sensed the darkness around her as if it was a living thing, a deep, dense fog.

She felt weighted down, the blood in her veins as heavy as lead. She tried to lift up her arm, to reach across the bed for Tanner, but even that simple movement was almost more than she could handle.

Her chest ached, her lungs clenching tightly, as if she'd run too far, too fast.

When she was finally able to stretch her arm out, she found the other side of the bed was empty.

She pried open her nearly sealed eyelids. With the heavy, light-deflecting curtains keeping out the sun and moon, she didn't even know if it was night or day, only that Tanner wasn't there with her.

And then it hit her, like a punch in the gut.

Of course Tanner isn't here. He sleeps on the couch in the living room.

It was true—he *had* relegated himself to the couch ever since she'd returned. She didn't think it was fair for him to give up his bed and she'd protested, but he pointed out that it used to be her bed, too, and with her being pregnant, she really needed the extra support.

She appreciated his thoughtfulness. Given that she didn't remember having married him, it seemed like the right thing to do.

But that wasn't what was bothering Rebecca right now.

It was *where* that thought—that Tanner was sleeping on the couch—had come from.

It had been a *memory*.

Something from *before*. But that made no sense.

Or maybe it did. She had, after all, been separated from him, even though with the relationship they now had, she couldn't imagine why.

Pain coursed through her body again and she curled into herself—or as much as she could being eight months pregnant. She felt as if someone had used her as a punching bag. Though physically she was fine, she was emotionally bruised and broken. Her baby protested, kicking at her ribs as Rebecca's stomach tightened uncontrollably.

Rebecca breathed in shallow pants as she'd been taught to do in the pregnancy-and-delivery class she and Tanner had just started the previous week. She still had a month to go before her baby was supposed to be born.

This couldn't be labor—could it?

Get a grip on yourself.

This wasn't labor, or even Braxton-Hicks contractions. The cramping wasn't focused, or even mostly centered on her belly. But it wasn't just a bad dream, either.

The biggest pain came from inside her chest.

Her heart.

She rolled onto her back and tried to relax and let her mind drift, but no other memories rose from her Swiss cheese brain. Just the feelings—*bad* feelings. Was this how it had been when she'd left Tanner?

The question now was *why?* What could have happened that would cause her to experience such a deep depression, for she was now convinced that's what she must have been feeling.

Something had set her off back then—something truly awful to make her feel like she was shrouded in darkness and was being pulled into the deep. What was it that had made her believe her only option was to separate from Tanner?

It was time to have a serious conversation with her husband and set things straight once and for all. She wanted the truth—the whole truth. She knew this about herself—she was a strong woman, and together with Tanner, they would get through whatever it was that had broken them apart the first time around.

Except now was the absolute worst conceivable time to have such a conversation. Tanner had enough on his plate since becoming Mackenzie's permanent guardian. His next step was adopting her. That took a lot of time and effort, talking to their lawyer and preparing all the paperwork, and that was nothing to say of the emotional battle he was fighting, knowing his sister had chosen jail over her own daughter.

He didn't need the added stress of Rebecca pressing him for details on their lives *before*.

Her curiosity, even as compelling as it was, would have to wait. Besides, it was the *after* that really counted, wasn't it? She couldn't imagine her life without Tanner now, and didn't even want to think about it.

She didn't care what had happened in the past. This time would be different.

The heaviness that had weighed her down when she'd first woken had now dissipated enough for her to get up and get dressed. She stretched out her cramped muscles and headed for the kitchen.

Things were complicated enough right now. She didn't want to be part of the problem. She wanted to be part of the solution. And she couldn't imagine the burden Tanner was carrying trying to provide for his ever-growing family.

Even though there was so much she didn't know about herself, she knew how much she wanted to be a mother. Every time she felt movement in her womb she rejoiced. She was also conscious that she used to love teaching middle school math—she had not only somehow retained those skills, but the passion for teaching kids had recently sparked to life.

"I've been thinking," she said to Tanner as she slid into her seat and buttered a piece of toast.

The puppy propped her front paws on Rebecca's knee and tilted her head in the most adorable fashion to beg for toast. To Tanner's chagrin, Mackenzie had chosen the name Sprinkles for the puppy. He'd already complained that there was no way to man up a name like Sprinkles.

Rebecca, however, loved the name—and the puppy. She couldn't resist Sprinkles's big brown eyes and broke off a corner of her toast to feed to the dog.

Tanner groaned. "It's bad enough that I have to face my friends with a dog named *Sprinkles* without you going and spoiling her that way."

Rebecca chuckled. "I'm sure your male ego will survive."

The corner of his lips curled up. "Says you."

"I eated all my eggs, Uncle Tanner," Mackenzie said, pointing at her empty plate. "Can I go play with Sprinkles now?"

"Put your plate in the sink and then yes, you may," Rebecca answered for him.

With the little girl gone and Peggy out for the day with her friends, it was just her and Tanner at the table.

"So, whatcha been thinking about?" Tanner said around a bite of bacon. He turned toward her as he spoke. When they'd first met after she'd returned to Serendipity, Tanner wouldn't even look at her face. Now he graced her with full-on eye contact and an open, friendly smile.

Was he finally learning to trust her?

More to the point—*should* he?

It frightened her that she didn't know.

"I...I remember that I used to teach math at the middle school," she stammered. "At least, I think it's a memory."

He nodded. "That's right. You used to love teaching. But—Rebecca, they had to replace you when you took off and didn't return after the winter holidays."

She couldn't maintain eye contact any longer. Shame washed over her, even if she wasn't precisely sure why.

"Yes, I know. Well, I figured as much. In any case, I couldn't go back to teaching school this year anyway. Not with our son due to be born next month. And there's Mackenzie to think about, as well. She'll be going to preschool in three weeks or so, but that's only half days three days a week. I need to be here for her when she is home."

"Your mom could help out."

"She could. But I don't know if you've noticed— she's tired. I would never insinuate that we are her caregivers, but I do want to be able to keep my eye on her and help her get the rest she needs."

"I'm fine with you staying home to raise the children," Tanner said bluntly. "I mean, if that's what you're worried about."

"No—that's not it. I do want to feel like I'm contributing more than I do."

"You don't think caring for the children is contributing?" He ran a hand across the muscles in his neck.

"Of course I do. But I also want the freedom to follow my passion projects. Taking care of the alpacas, of course. And teaching math. I thought I could hang out my shingle and do some tutoring for middle and high school students. I like the idea of it being one-on-one, although I could probably handle small groups, as well."

"Are you sure you're not pushing yourself too hard, Rebecca? You were just in a life-changing accident a few months ago."

She frowned and studied his expression. His words hadn't come out as overbearing and he didn't sound like he was trying to talk her out of anything. He was just anxious.

"You don't think it's a good idea to start my own business? I don't know why, but the thought of being an entrepreneur appeals to me. I bought a few books on my e-reader and am researching all the details of how to go into business for myself."

He gave a low whistle.

"What?"

"I'm impressed, is all. You aren't letting your amnesia hold you back anymore. I always knew you had a strong will. I'm happy to see you didn't lose it in the accident."

"So that's a good thing, then?"

He reached across the table and grabbed her hand. "Not good, Rebecca. Great. I'm 100 percent behind you on whatever dreams you want to chase, as long as—"

He couldn't finish his sentence. He brushed a hand across his jaw, refusing to continue.

He didn't have to. Rebecca could see it in his eyes. *As long as she didn't leave him again.*

Chapter Twelve

Tanner leaned his shoulder on the doorjamb between the kitchen and the dining room and watched his wife work. It had been two weeks since they'd had the discussion about her opening her own business. She had several business and accounting books stacked on the table, as well as a number of government forms she'd filled out and needed to go over with her lawyer before officially hanging out her Mighty Math Tutoring sign on the community boards at the high school and middle school.

Not that she really needed to advertise. Word of mouth was by far the best form of advertising, and it was free. All they'd had to do was mention to Jo Spencer at Cup O' Jo's Café that she was looking for students and she'd already gotten a deluge of phone calls from eager parents and students.

Of course, the baby would come first. She intended to take six weeks off just to enjoy their son before she started working as a tutor, but she wanted to have all her ducks in a row so that when the time came to open her business, all she'd have to do was turn the proverbial sign from Closed to Open.

That was his Rebecca. Planning every aspect so there was nothing left to chance.

Tanner smiled, seeing her so happy. There was a glow about her that only partly had to do with her pregnancy. Anything that made Rebecca's heart warm automatically made Tanner's heart do the same.

At the moment, she was clicking through a financial program on her laptop and filling numbers in the boxes. She was totally focused on her spreadsheet.

He desperately wanted to swing her chair around and kiss her. Those feelings reminded him of when they'd first started dating in their early twenties.

He approached her from behind and rubbed her shoulders, which were tense from stooping over her computer. "How's my entrepreneur feeling today?"

She nearly jumped out of her seat at his touch.

"You scared ten years off my life," she said, stretching her neck from side to side to relieve the muscle strain. "I was starting to feel a little sleepy and was getting ready to take a break, maybe a little catnap, but now you've got my adrenaline going again. You move so quietly you should come with a warning bell around your neck."

"Sorry. I figured you knew I was there. I didn't realize you were so lost in thought."

She leaned back and smiled at him. "Just enjoying crunching all my numbers for my new business."

He laughed and shook his head. "Only a math geek

would say something like that." He kissed the top of her head affectionately.

"I beg your pardon?" she teased.

"Kidding, not kidding," he replied, his grin widening as he bobbed his eyebrows. "As it happens, I have a thing for math geeks."

"I guess that's a good thing, then, since you married one."

Their eyes met and held, her gaze sparkling with mirth—and something else. Tanner swallowed hard.

"And our future football player? How's he doing today? Still moving around a lot in there?"

His question had been light but earnest, and her gaze changed from joy to perplexity and she shook her head slightly as if in confusion.

He lowered his brow. "What?"

"It's probably nothing."

"No, you don't get to do that. You can't close up on me. Tell me what you're thinking."

He sounded desperate even to his own ears. But he knew firsthand how easy a relationship went from some small burr under the saddle to an enormous infection even the best medicine couldn't fix.

He remembered that impassable ravine that had once formed between them, and he would do whatever it took to make sure that never happened again.

He would gently pick the burr out *now*.

"It's just that you ask me about the baby moving several times every day, even though nothing's really changed. *I'm* having trouble moving. I feel like a beached whale. But our son is doing fine, and I'm beginning to get paranoid every time you ask about our baby. What are you not telling me?"

He suddenly felt woozy and was unable to catch a breath. His knees buckling, and his gaze tunneling, he scrambled for the chair next to Rebecca and just barely crashed into the seat without falling to the floor.

She reached for his arm. "Are you okay?"

He forced a breath in to his lungs and then let it out slowly. "I'm fine."

Then he jammed both hands back through his thick blond hair and modified his statement. "No, Rebecca, I'm *not* fine. I've—we've—been putting off this conversation for far too long. Your memory appears to be returning in bits and pieces, and to be honest, I've been walking around dreading the moment when you remember everything again."

"Because I left you?" she asked gently. "And you're afraid that whatever it was that broke us apart the first time will do so again?"

"Yes," he said, but he was shaking his head even as the word came out of his mouth. "No. I mean, obviously, that's important. But there is—so much more. I—I warn you—this is going to hurt. That was one of the reasons I kept putting off talking about it—I wasn't sure you were physically and emotionally up to hearing it. But that's not the only reason, or even the major one. The larger obstacle, I'm ashamed to say, is that I'm being selfish. I need you to stay with me, especially now that we have Mackenzie and the new baby coming."

"And you think if I know—whatever it is you're

about to tell me, I'm going to leave, the same way I did the first time?"

He scoffed and shrugged. "Maybe."

"If you're going to be completely honest, then I will be, as well. There have been mornings recently when I've woken up and I feel like I have a dark, heavy cloud settled over me. It's hard for me to move."

Tanner lowered his head and groaned.

"Tell me something," Rebecca said, scooting her chair until she was facing him and then tipping up his chin until their eyes met. "The relationship we have now, the one we've been building here together—is it *real*? Because to me, it feels like we're a family. That we're successfully working toward regaining a husband-and-wife relationship."

He swallowed twice through a dry throat. "Me, too. Better even than I imagined it might be when we stood at the altar and you took—"

"I took what?" she asked curiously.

"I was going to say, *my name*, but now you don't remember yourself as Rebecca Hamilton, only as Rebecca Foster."

"That's not exactly true," she admitted. "It's like how I was telling you about waking up with feelings I don't know how to categorize. But there's been more than that. I think my memories are returning, Tanner. Just tiny bits here and there at this point and I don't have everything I need to give them context, but I'm starting to be able to piece some things together. I don't know if it *is* my memory coming back, or just me settling into my role here as your wife, but I do think of myself as Rebecca Hamilton."

Tears pricked at his eyes. It had meant the world to him when she'd elected to take his name the day they were married. That she'd done so again right now made his heart warm beyond measure.

If only he didn't have to ruin it with his next words.

"We need to talk about the baby," he said, deciding that putting it off any longer was just going to cause both of them further pain.

Rebecca put a protective hand over her belly and rubbed at the sudden rounded bump that rose up to meet it. She smiled softly. "This kid thinks my rib is a swing set. I can't even imagine how active he is going to be. We're going to be running all over chasing after him. I picture him climbing bookcases and sliding down the stairs headfirst while we chase along behind."

"You'll never know how good it is to hear that. Can I—?"

She reached for his hand and put his palm down next to her left ribs. Sure enough, his son—*their* son—was doing jumping jacks in her womb.

Thank you, Jesus.

"Be straight with me," Rebecca urged. "Why is it that you keep asking me if our son is active? At first I thought it was just a daddy thing—you wanting your son to be good at sports or whatever—although personally, I have to admit I'm rooting for math geek or student body president."

He knew she was trying to lighten the moment, but she didn't yet understand the gravity of what he was about to say and he just couldn't bring himself to crack a smile.

"So if it isn't our son's amazing football career you're encouraging, or that you're sure he's going to find the cure for cancer, what *did* you want to talk to me about?"

Tanner stared at her for a moment, his eyes wide with confusion, before he finally realized she'd mistakenly believed that when he'd said they needed to talk about the baby, he was speaking about the child currently in her womb and not the one they'd lost.

"There was—" His voice cracked and he coughed to dislodge the emotions in his throat. "There was another baby, Rebecca. We had another child together. A daughter."

"We had a—a—?" She pushed back from the table, away from him, her gaze instantly filling with tears. "I don't understand. What do you mean we *had* a daughter? What happened to her?"

"She—she was stillborn. We lost her at seven months."

"That can't be true," she said, vigorously shaking her head as her face turned an alarming shade of red. "I would remember that!"

He didn't blame her for being angry. It wasn't directed at him—yet. It was only a matter of time, though, before she did turn her anger upon him.

It had taken him at least a year to come to grips with losing their child. Of being angry with God for allowing it to happen, so much so that at one point he'd felt as if his faith had been ripped out of him along with his heart.

What good did it do to be the protector and provider of his family if he couldn't even save his daughter, if he couldn't reach his wife before she'd disappeared down the deep, dark hole of depression?

And now, to have to revisit it all—he'd thought he'd come to grips with everything, but his grief had never really completely disappeared. He'd just managed to tuck most of it away in the back of his heart, only for it to reemerge now.

"That doesn't even make any sense," she continued when he didn't answer her—because he didn't *have* an answer for her.

"Some things in life simply don't have a rational answer, sweetheart," he murmured. "If there's one thing I've learned from all this, it's that in those moments, we have to let God take the reins. We will never know why our precious daughter was taken from us—at least until we see our Lord in Heaven. But now He's given us Mackenzie. Not as a replacement for our daughter, but as another child to love."

She rubbed her temples with her fingers and then pinched the bridge of her nose so hard she left a mark. "I still don't get it. This isn't the Middle Ages, and I was at a hospital, right? Lots of babies are born healthy at seven months. Even if their little lungs need a bit more time to develop, they have NICUs full of special equipment. Even if our baby—if she—was born premature, why didn't she live?" She was almost shouting now.

He tried to reach for her hand but she snatched it away and tucked both hands over her belly.

Tanner's heart was being sliced apart shred by painful shred. "Our daughter—we named her Faith Rebecca Hamilton—had already passed away in the womb. The doctor said she'd been gone for days by the time you went into labor. There was truly nothing the doctors and nurses could have done to save her."

To his surprise, Rebecca looked him straight in the eye. "Tell me about her. Everything you remember."

"You want me to—?" He swiped a hand down his face to clear away the moisture. He wasn't certain he could do this.

She nodded. "I need to know."

"She was beautiful. Amazing. Ten perfectly formed tiny fingers and ten tiny toes. She had—she had the cutest little button nose you ever did see. Just like on her five-month ultrasound. She had a tuft of auburn hair just like yours.

"We didn't know what was wrong at first." Tanner frowned as he remembered the way the doctor had avoided his questions. "The doctor didn't say anything for a long time. He handed Faith off to a nurse, who quickly wrapped her in a blanket. At first I thought she was just swaddling our daughter, and I remember holding my breath, waiting to hear the baby give her first precious wail.

"But that didn't happen. And it didn't look to me like the nurse was trying to do very much to help the baby breathe. She just stared down at her as she held her. Everything seemed like it was in slow motion.

"I started to feel like something was up and stared closely at the doctor's expression. He wouldn't look at me, but just went on about his business. That's when I knew for sure something was wrong."

He ran a hand down his jaw. "I think you figured

it out before I did. You were so exhausted after your hours of labor, but you kept yelling, 'Where's my baby? What's wrong with my baby?'" A frustrated growl emerged from the back of his throat. "Your voice… those words…they haunt me to this day."

Rebecca sniffled and dabbed at her tears with the back of one hand, while simultaneously reaching out for his hand with the other.

"We took turns holding her for the longest time. The nurses said we could have all the time we needed to say goodbye. It was so hard to let her go."

He squeezed her hand, wondering how to continue, because from that moment onward everything in their lives had tanked. He now realized he'd made Rebecca's depression worse by not believing depression was even a real thing. He had dealt with his grief in a different way—by working nonstop.

"You weren't able to bounce back from that tragedy," he said. "You became very depressed and stayed in bed all day. You wouldn't eat anything and lost a lot of weight."

"That part, I remember. Well, not all of it. But sometimes when I wake up in the morning I experience flashbacks that I assume must be what depression feels like. I don't ever want to go back to that horrible place."

"Me, neither. I was so frustrated."

"With me?"

"Partially. But mostly with myself. I couldn't figure out how to help you. Nothing I did seemed to work. I couldn't reach you, and you wanted to have nothing to do with me."

"So you did—what?"

"Dealt with my grief in my own way. Worked from sunup to well after sundown. Tried not to bother you. Slept on the couch."

"Hmm. And then at some point I decided I'd had enough and I left?"

He nodded soberly. "Eventually you must have started getting better, but by that time we were living completely separate lives. We never talked or tried to work anything out. I didn't know what was going on with you, and you didn't tell me. Instead, I came home one evening and found you gone. No note or anything."

"And that's the end of the story?"

"No. You called me once, but I was so hurt and so bitter I hung up on you. I think you were going to tell me you were pregnant with our son. I didn't see or hear from you again until you showed up at the auction in Serendipity."

Rebecca sighed heavily. "That's a lot to take in."

"I know. I hope this doesn't send you spiraling backward. But I couldn't put off telling you any longer."

"No. We needed to have this conversation," she agreed. "But now that we have, I think we've hit a brick wall."

"What does that mean?"

"It means," Rebecca said, hiccuping a sob between short breaths, "we have some big decisions to make. Like where do we go from here?"

"I'm sorry, Tanner. I—I've got to get out of here for a bit. I need some fresh air and some time to think."

He let out a breath and nodded, his unblinking gaze full of pain. "I understand."

Rebecca couldn't remain in the kitchen any longer. She couldn't watch the broken expression on Tanner's face any longer and know that—at least partially—she had been the one to put it there. His presence was just too painful for her to bear.

And it must be so much worse for him. She couldn't imagine how he could stand to be in the same room with her after everything that had happened.

Not after what she'd done to him. She couldn't even meet his gaze, she was so ashamed of her actions. He was clearly feeling her betrayal all over again, while she was trying to wrap her head around everything that had led up to their separation as if for the first time.

What they'd suffered together would have put enormous pressure on any young couple. It was the type of make-or-break experience where a marriage either emerged from the trial stronger than ever or suffered from complete brokenness that would eventually rip a husband and wife apart.

Evidently, she and Tanner had somehow fallen into the latter category.

And that was what confused her most of all.

During the past few months, she and Tanner had built a stable relationship based on friendship and respect. She didn't know how he felt, but there was no question she was experiencing romantic feelings for him, as well.

She admired his work ethic, and more than that, his work/life balance. He somehow managed to complete his ranch work and still be there for most meals—he even cooked some of them, which was something Rebecca didn't remember from before, although, granted, there were still big holes where her memory should be.

But Tanner's integrity, the way he took care of Mackenzie and openly showed his love for her, the way he and Rebecca laughed together and sometimes talked long into the night—this wasn't the kind of man any woman in her right mind would choose to leave.

Her head ached as she pressed into her memory.

So why had she left?

Instead of taking a walk, she quietly closed the door to her bedroom and slipped into the attached bathroom to splash some cold water on her face. Her eyes were red and bloodshot from all the crying she'd done, and she suspected she wasn't finished. Her heart was in so much pain it physically hurt to move.

She let the water run to ice and then cupped her hands and brought it to her face, splashing the cold liquid over her hot, stinging eyes.

Dear Lord, help me to have clarity. Where am I supposed to go from here?

She didn't have answers. She wasn't even sure what the questions were anymore.

She'd firmly believed the Lord had led her back into Tanner's life. God had given them a special blessing with their baby growing in her womb—a child Rebecca deeply felt deserved to be raised by both a mother and a father. Not only that, but Tanner was determined to take full custody of Mackenzie. A husband-and-wife team would look much better on paper and facing a judge—

far, far better than a single cowboy, for sure, even if he was her only living blood relative apart from Lydia.

She couldn't turn away from those obligations.

She didn't *want* to.

But the question was, would Tanner want *her*, now that her memories were returning? Or would he slip back into his old ways, hiding out on the ranch and choosing not to work through the difficulties in their relationship?

Would they ever be husband and wife again?

Chapter Thirteen

Tanner picked up a bale of hay in each hand and hauled them from the barn to the alpaca pen, setting them down only long enough to open the gate.

Sprinkles appeared at his ankle, barking and turning in circles, clearly wanting to join in the fun.

Presumably, Mackenzie was thinking of baking cookies with sprinkles when she'd come up with that name, but the puppy had put her own mark on it. House-training was seriously high on the family's to-do list.

He stood back and gestured at the puppy. "Do you want to come in and practice your herding skills?"

Sprinkles barked and pounced forward a few steps, but as soon as the nearest alpaca moved, the puppy bounded back to safety on the outside of the fence.

Tanner sighed. "Yeah, that's what I thought. You're only brave when there's a fence between you and the herd. You'll learn, though, and despite your unfortunate name, I think you'll eventually be a really big help to me."

Sprinkles jumped onto Tanner's leg, her tongue lolling to one side, begging for affection. He couldn't help but laugh and scratch the dog between the ears.

"Yeah, yeah, I remember. *You* picked *me*."

He pulled the hay bales inside the fence line and broke up some of it with his gloved hands, spreading it along the ground while the alpacas honked indignantly at him to leave their sanctuary.

"I'm bringing you food," he protested, ruffling Brownie's mop hairdo when she got right up in his face. "I would think you'd be more appreciative."

Brownie responded by head-bumping his arm.

"All right, already. You guys need to work on being more grateful toward the hand that feeds you. This is hard work, you know. You think I do this for my health?"

His only answer was increased honking, although a few of the herd had lost interest in him with the advent of breakfast.

The only human being the alpacas really responded to was Rebecca. She'd spent a great deal of time out in the field with them since she'd come back to Serendipity. They'd gotten to know her, and she was now a walking, talking alpaca encyclopedia. If anything, she loved her herd more now than when she'd originally gotten the cockeyed notion to purchase them in the first place.

At first, Tanner thought it was because she felt obligated toward them because he'd told her the herd was there because of her. But once she'd started learning about them and then attending a couple of activities, she'd become hooked. Or rehooked, as the case may be.

The truth was, she appeared to love everything about

ranch living. Far more than during their first few years of marriage.

What she didn't appear so sure about was what she intended to do regarding her relationship with him.

It had been a week since he'd come clean about their stillborn daughter. There hadn't been the major reconciliation he'd hoped for, a coming together in sharing mutual grief so they could then move forward as a couple. On the other hand, she hadn't left him again, nor did she give him any reason to expect she might.

He was still afraid honesty might put an end to their relationship, but at least he wasn't carrying around the burden of secrecy and guilt anymore. Everything was out in the open. Now it was up to Rebecca what she wanted to do with what she now knew.

She wasn't avoiding him, exactly. They were simply tiptoeing around the serious issues and keeping the tone of their conversations entirely casual. Her short-term memory had returned in full and she appeared to enjoy her days playing with Mackenzie and planning her tutoring business.

But even though they didn't talk about it, the ravine was there, staring them both in the face.

They were a husband and wife who weren't a husband and wife.

He couldn't really blame her for the way she was acting toward him. She already had a lot on her mind, what with the baby due in a week. She assured him at least six times a day that their son was still active and kicking up a storm. He appreciated the effort she went to in order to encourage him, but now he felt like he must have appeared really overbearing with his daily questions for her to respond in such a way.

Or maybe, now that she had the whole picture, she was just as frightened as he was.

And he *was* frightened, in more ways than one. With nothing resolved and a baby coming, Tanner could think of little else but the questionable status of his relationship with Rebecca. Would they become the family he longed for, or would he end up being part-time father to his son?

When he returned to the barn to muck out the stalls and feed the horses, he found Rebecca in Calypso's stall, brushing her mare and carrying on a one-sided conversation. He stopped dead in his tracks, not sure exactly why he didn't approach her, but not wanting to make his presence known just yet.

Maybe it was simply that he loved the deep, rich alto tone of Rebecca's voice when she spoke to the animals.

Or maybe it was because as soon as he stepped into the barn, he heard his own name being spoken.

"I've never been more confused in my life," she admitted to Calypso. "You're lucky you're a horse and don't have to deal with stallions all the time. That gets confusing fast, doesn't it? I'll tell you the truth, Calypso. I don't have the slightest idea what to do in my relationship with Tanner."

That was for sure. Tanner felt exactly the same way. Walking on eggshells, afraid to say the wrong words.

"At least the baby is cooperating. I started panicking after Tanner told me about what happened with our daughter. But our son's movements haven't slowed down at all, even though I read in a book that they might slow down right before I go into labor. And I had an extra ultrasound, just to reassure myself everything was good. It is, thank the Lord."

Tanner hadn't realized she'd had another ultrasound. He wondered why she didn't think to tell him about it. His gut clenched. Maybe they weren't on the same page, as he'd thought they were. Because even if everything in their lives was up in the air, there were certain things they ought to be sharing with each other—most especially like doctor's visits concerning their son.

He was considering how to announce his presence when Rebecca continued.

"But then again, things are getting more complicated than ever. I'm so afraid to say anything to Tanner at all. I don't know, Calypso. Do you think I should tell him?"

"Tell me what?"

Rebecca squeaked and the bristle brush she was holding went flying.

She turned on him with a frown on her face, propping her fists on her hips. "How many times do I have to ask you not to do that?" she demanded.

He shrugged and offered a reticent half smile. "Sorry."

"You should be. I'm already only going to live to be forty because of all the times you've scared ten years off my life. If you keep doing that, I'm going to end up in negative numbers pretty soon. Although losing a few years wouldn't be too bad, I suppose. Oh, to be young, pretty and innocent again."

"I—I wouldn't want you to change a thing," he admitted. "Love grows stronger through trials. I think you're more beautiful than ever."

She flushed. "Well, thank you for that. But I'm still going to look into investing in a bell."

He nodded. "I think if we've learned anything from what we've been through, it's that young and innocent will only take you so far."

"Agreed."

"So what were you talking about when I came in?"

"That was a private conversation between me and my horse, thank you very much."

He could tell by the tone of her voice that she was teasing, so he gathered his courage to address the elephant in the room. Elephants didn't belong in a stable with horses.

"I heard my name. You were saying you didn't know whether or not you should tell me something. I hope by now you know you can trust me. There're things I pray you'll never feel it's necessary to say, but there's nothing you *can't* say to me. Do you know what I mean?"

She nodded, her brow furrowing. "Yes. I know. I feel the same way. You should always feel free to speak to me about anything."

He leaned his forearms against Calypso's stall door and waited for her to start talking.

She didn't immediately speak. Instead, she reached down and picked up the bristle brush, sliding it evenly across Calypso's flank.

"I went to see Dr. Delia this morning."

Should he admit he'd heard that part or stay silent about it? In the end, he compromised.

"I see," he said, but it came out husky and he cleared his throat.

"I was going to ask you to come along with me but I couldn't find you. I think you were out checking on the cattle. I tried calling your cell phone but it rang from the couch cushion and I realized you must have forgotten to take it with you. I would have waited, but Dr. Delia only had that one early appointment today and I didn't want to put it off any longer."

Tanner let out a long, silent breath and his heart filled with warmth. She hadn't purposely left him out after all. There was a more logical explanation. He had been with the cattle and had forgotten his cell phone.

"So what did you find out?"

"Our little guy is just exactly right on schedule. He looked great. And Delia checked me and said it wouldn't be long now. I'm excited, but terrified."

Every male instinct in him wanted to hold her in his arms, to let her know she wasn't alone in this, wouldn't be alone *ever*. He couldn't have the baby for her, but he'd be right by her side holding her hand.

He clicked open the stall door and slipped in, holding his arms out to her.

For a moment, she didn't move. Then she made a delicate sound from the back of her throat and buried her face in his chest, clutching the front of his shirt in both fists.

He wrapped his arms around her and hugged her tightly.

"I know," he admitted. "I am, too. But we made a

birthing plan and took those classes, so I think we're as ready as we'll ever be. And I'm excited to meet our son."

She leaned back and met his gaze. "Me, too. But—"

He waited for her to finish her sentence but she didn't.

"But what?" he finally asked.

"There's still so much in our relationship that needs to be worked out."

"I know, but it doesn't have to be done overnight, does it? Sure, we're a little behind, what with the amnesia and all, but we'll always be working on our relationship. I don't think that ever really stops," he said thoughtfully. "Successful couples are always working on their relationships, talking out their problems, growing closer to each other and supporting one another. Taking care of children together will also serve to bring us closer together if we let it."

"That's true. And that's the way I'd like us to be."

His heart soared to hear those words and it was all he could do not to punch a fist of victory in the air. The fear he'd been carrying with him for so long dissipated at last. She wasn't going to abandon him again. She wanted to work on their relationship. Praise God!

"But—"

Oh, no. There was a *but*.

He stiffened, not wanting to hear the rest of the statement.

She stepped back, her eyes glistening. "But I don't think we're yet at the point where we can start today and move forward, do you? We've still got a lot of baggage to deal with from our past, and it's pretty major."

He brushed that stubborn lock of hair out of her eyes and then framed her face with his palms. "Isn't that what we've been doing?"

She blinked away a tear. "Yes. Except—" she swept in an audible breath "—except I haven't told you everything."

A million different scenarios, none of them good, immediately crossed his mind.

What hadn't she told him?

"What do you mean?" he choked out.

"My memories," she whispered hoarsely. "After we talked about Faith, my long-term memories came flooding back. I told you I'd been experiencing…emotions that I didn't know how to classify. I understand now I was suffering from major depression. It really frightened me when I woke up the other day and couldn't move because my body was so weighted down. The darkness is terrifying. I was living inside that, Tanner. Every day. I reached out to you but you weren't there."

"I know. I handled that all wrong. At first I didn't understand it. I honestly didn't think depression was a real thing. But when you continued to remain secluded and lost too much weight, I really started to worry."

"Then why—?"

"Why didn't I get you help?" he interrupted. "Because I'm an idiot with too much pride to admit it when he's done something wrong."

She shook her head, but not enough to release his palms. "That's not the man I see when I look at you."

"I hope not. If these trials have done anything, they've made me realize experiencing emotions—and showing them—doesn't make me less of a man. I had a lot to confess to God, but with His help, I think I'm a better man for it all."

"No question. You were there for Mackenzie when she needed you. You were there for me—which frankly, now that I have all my memories back, kind of surprises me. I wasn't very nice to you."

"You were hurting."

"Still. I pushed you away."

"And I went. I lost myself in ranch work instead of taking care of you as I should have."

"So," she said, locking her gaze with his. "Now I know everything—*feel* everything. And I know that you know. The question is, can our relationship truly survive all we've been through? Or do we go our separate ways?"

They stared at each other for a long time without speaking. Tanner's breath lodged painfully in his throat. He'd known all along it was going to come down to this moment eventually, but now that it was here, he wasn't ready. He wanted to run away with his fingers covering his ears so he couldn't hear her answer to the question he had yet to ask.

He took a deep breath and spit out the words that would change his life forever.

"What do you want?"

Rebecca narrowed her gaze on him. Now that her long-term memories had returned, she knew just how bad things had been between them before she'd left. She understood why she'd felt the only way to heal her heart had been to leave, how she'd had to get away in order to straighten out her thoughts and emotions.

She knew why Dawn, her best friend since childhood and the woman who had opened her house to Rebecca, hadn't gone with her that day in Serendipity. Because Dawn didn't want her to return. She had never liked Tanner. Since the day Tanner first asked Rebecca out, Dawn had been jealous of him, of the time he took away from their friendship. And when Tanner and Rebecca had become engaged, he had become her new best friend, nudging Dawn into second place in Rebecca's life.

That was what growing up was all about, but Dawn had never understood. And the truth was, Rebecca had known Dawn's negative feelings about Tanner and had gone to stay at Dawn's house anyway. Part of it had been that she really didn't have anyplace else to go, and part of it was that Dawn didn't live too far from Serendipity, so when the time was right, Rebecca could return to her real home.

Looking back on it with fresh insight, the idea to stay with Dawn had been a very foolish choice on her part, because from the very first day she was there, Dawn had encouraged a permanent separation from Tanner, had insisted Rebecca was better off without him.

That had never been Rebecca's intention.

When she'd made her vows to Tanner, they had been forever. She just needed some time apart to heal her heart after losing Faith, and then she'd return and work things out with her marriage. It was too overwhelming to do both at once.

Except that's not what had happened. She'd made the decision to return to Tanner and had even packed her suitcases. She was on a final run to the store for a few last-minute items when she'd been sideswiped by a drunk driver and had lost her memory. Thank God her son had been cocooned in her womb and had somehow not suffered from the accident.

But Rebecca had. She'd lost every memory, every moment of time going back to her high school years. She'd been shocked to see her driver's license listed her as Rebecca Hamilton and not Rebecca Foster.

Rebecca had to press on Dawn to tell her the whole truth, but at length she'd learned she had a husband, and a life, in Serendipity, Texas, where she'd grown up.

From that moment on, her focus had been on discovering her past and finding her memories. Yet that wasn't all that had happened while she explored her old/new world at the ranch.

She'd made new memories, and a new life, with Tanner and Mackenzie, in a beautiful, happy home. Even better, their son was due any day now, which would be a blessing beyond compare.

And now Tanner was asking her if she wanted to leave.

"Why would you ask that?" she whispered, her voice dry and husky. She dropped her eyes, unable to meet his gaze.

"Because it has to be your choice. I need to hear those words, Rebecca. We've been through so much together and I—I need to know you aren't going to run away again."

Was that what he thought? That she'd run away every time things got rough? What about all the time they'd spent together recently, the way their relationship had bloomed from newfound friendship into love—at least on her side.

Did that count for nothing?

Did he still not trust her?

"Please don't," she begged, squeezing her eyes shut against the tears flowing down her face. She'd meant to say, *Please don't worry*, but her throat had closed around the last word and she hadn't been able to get it out.

Tanner dropped his arms to his sides, his hands in fists, and stepped back. "If that's what you want, Rebecca. I won't pressure you to make a decision."

Her gaze widened.

"No. No! That's not what I meant at all."

His gaze narrowed. "What, then?"

"What I meant to say," she said, focusing on enunciating every word, "is don't *worry*. I have all my memories back, and I can assure you I'm not the same woman I was when I separated from you."

"No. You're not."

"And you are not the same man. We've both suffered, but we've also found joy, and we have a lot to look forward to together."

"Together?" His voice was so full of hope Rebecca thought her heart might burst. She could no longer wait to tell him what was in her heart.

She gazed up at him and caressed his cheek. "I love you, Tanner. I never stopped, not even when things were at their worst. There's nothing more important than what we've built together here, as a couple and as a family. I am committed to that, and I am committed to you. Now and forever."

"Now and forever," he echoed, his lips mere inches above hers. She placed her palm on his chest, over his heart, delighting in the way it pounded in rhythm with hers. She closed her eyes, feeling the warmth of his breath on her cheek, and inhaled the outdoor scent that was distinctly Tanner.

Finally, she was right where she belonged.

Home.

Chapter Fourteen

Tanner kissed her for the longest time, completely immersed in the love he felt for his wife. His beautiful, talented, wonderful wife.

He reached for both of her hands and squeezed them and then ran his palms up to her shoulders, locking their gazes.

"This moment is so significant, I feel like I ought to be down on one knee offering you a ring along with my heart."

"I already have a ring."

"Yes, but you don't wear it."

"Only because my left hand had been in a splint all this time and my fingers were too swollen for me to wear a ring. But that doesn't mean I don't carry it with me everywhere I go."

She reached up to her neck and revealed a silver chain, on which was looped her engagement solitaire and her marriage band. She released the clasp on the necklace and slid the rings into her palm.

Tanner's heart was so large he thought it might explode. "How are your fingers now? Do you think the rings will fit?"

"There's one way to find out." She reached for his hand and carefully transferred the rings from her grasp to his.

He grinned and dropped to one knee. "I've never been one to pass up a good opportunity. Rebecca Constance Foster Hamilton, would you do me the very great honor of consenting to—to continue being my beloved wife? Will you embrace Mackenzie into our family just as you do now and love her as I do? Will you rejoice with me at the birth of our son? Will you be mine now and forever?"

Rebecca held out her left hand, her eyes glimmering with tears as a smile spread across her face. "I can think of nothing I would like more in this whole wide world."

They both gave an audible sigh when the rings slid on easily.

"Whew. I was a little worried about that," he admitted, rising to his feet. "What if I had made that huge declaration and then the rings didn't fit? That would have been rather anticlimactic, don't you think?"

She made a funny face—not funny, really, but something between a smile and a wince—and then her gaze widened to epic proportions.

He raised his eyebrows. "What was that?"

Rebecca took a deep breath and her smile returned in earnest.

"If I'm not mistaken, my water just broke."

Tanner felt a moment of panic. "Is the baby still moving?"

"Not as much this morning, but that is normal for

right before delivery. I still feel his heel from time to time. Nothing to worry about."

But he could tell she was worried, too.

"It's only thirty-eight weeks."

"That's considered full-term. Our son is fine. However, we do need to start thinking about calling Dr. Delia and getting to the hospital."

"What? Oh. R-right. Call Dr. Delia. Get to the hospital," he echoed, his voice tight and squeaky.

Rebecca laughed. Considering she was the one having the baby, Tanner was certainly the more agitated of the two of them. She looked calm and focused.

"You see if you can get ahold of Dr. Delia," Rebecca instructed.

"I'm on it. I have her emergency number. This is definitely an emergency."

"No, it's not. It's perfectly natural."

"I can't help but—" He swallowed hard.

"This baby isn't Faith," she reminded him quickly. "I'm going to need you to be positive right now. You're my coach and I'll need all the support I can get."

Tanner squared his shoulders and focused his mind. "Of course. Your suitcase for the hospital is already packed and in the cab of the truck. Go change your clothes and then I'll meet you there, okay? Don't forget to keep track of your contractions."

Rebecca laughed. "I won't."

Tanner pulled out his cell phone and called Dr. Delia, who promised she'd meet them at the hospital. She had him describe what he'd seen and how bad he thought the contractions were.

"It didn't look like she was in too much pain," he said. "She wasn't doubling over or anything."

"I think you may very well have caught her very first contraction. Labor will likely take hours," Delia assured him. "You have plenty of time to get to the hospital and get Rebecca comfortable with an epidural before her contractions get too painful."

That was it. Tanner had a mission. He didn't want to see Rebecca in pain. They'd decided in their birth plan that she'd have an epidural, so the sooner he could get her to the hospital, the better.

He jogged into the house, calling frantically for Peggy. She dashed down the stairs, an excited smile on her face.

"Rebecca," Tanner said, panting as if he'd run a long distance. Really, it was just panic causing him to hyperventilate. "She's in labor."

"I know. She just talked to me. Take a breath, Tanner. Everything is going to be all right this time."

"I know. I'm just—overexcited, I guess."

"We all are, honey. Now you just focus on getting your wife to the hospital safely, okay? Jo Spencer is on her way over to watch Mackenzie, so I'll be along shortly. Just remember what you learned in birthing class. The most important thing you can do is just be there for her, offering as much or as little support as she needs at any given moment."

He frowned. "As little?"

"Exactly. There may be times when she says or does things that could hurt your ego. Don't let it. This is all about her and delivering a healthy baby."

"Right." Tanner nodded.

He could do this. He *had* to do this.

"But don't take too much time to get there, huh?" He could still hear Peggy laughing as he went out the front door.

Rebecca was already waiting in the cab when he got there.

"Have you been counting your contractions? How many have you had? How long are they? Are they very far apart? I have a notebook and pen you can use to keep track of the times until we get to the hospital."

"Well, look at you, Mr. Birth Coach, all organized and everything."

He scrubbed a hand through his hair. "Ugh. Don't tease me. I have to do what I can to feel like I have even just the littlest bit of control here."

"I know. Actually, I've only had two contractions after the first one. Neither was very long and weren't really painful. I think we have plenty of time to get to the hospital."

"That's what Dr. Delia said. But buckle up, because this pregnancy transport is going to hit the highway."

By the time they made it to the hospital an hour later, Rebecca's contractions were coming in earnest. They were still not completely regular, but they were coming a bit closer together and were definitely more painful.

Tanner started to turn into the emergency parking but Rebecca stopped him.

"Stork parking, remember?"

"I know, but you—"

"Will be fine for the amount of time it will take us to get up to the maternity ward. This way we can go straight up and bypass the regular hospital triage."

Tanner parked as close to the door as possible and raced around the front end of the truck to help Rebecca out before she'd even had the chance to open the passenger-side door. He clutched one of her hands and kept an arm firmly around her waist to support her.

"I can walk," she informed him with a chuckle. But right then, a particularly bad contraction hit and she stopped in her tracks, clinging to Tanner's hand as she breathed through the pain.

"Right," Tanner said as soon as the contraction was over. "I'm not leaving your side, and that's that."

She didn't argue with him again. With great excitement and a little bit of trepidation, they took the elevator to Mercy Medical's maternity ward. Rebecca was immediately whisked off to triage while Tanner was held back to fill out some papers, even though they'd done most of that in the preview packet.

Dr. Delia met Tanner at the nurses' station and they went into the triage unit to find Rebecca all hooked up to wires.

Tanner turned as white as a sheet and grabbed for Rebecca's hand.

"What's wrong?" he asked, his voice high and tight. He was addressing his question both to Rebecca and Dr. Delia.

The ladies looked at each other and laughed.

Tanner's face went from white to red. "What?"

"Don't panic," Dr. Delia assured him. "This is just

a fetal monitor. It's telling us what your son is doing."
She led him up to a machine that had scribbling needles
and was spitting out paper.

"This looks like a lie-detector test," Tanner said.

"It does, kind of, doesn't it? See these long squiggles?
Those are the contractions. When they start to get really
close together, we'll know it's time to start pushing."

The nurses unstrapped Rebecca from all the wires
and checked her into a nice, bright-colored room.

"When does she get the epidural?" Tanner asked anxiously, as Rebecca doubled over with another contraction.

"The anesthesiologist is on his way. Hang in there."

Thankfully, it didn't take long to get Rebecca settled comfortably in bed with her epidural. The nurse
suggested Tanner go get a sandwich from the cafeteria
while Rebecca rested, but he refused, saying there was
no way he could eat.

Rebecca's mom arrived and they took turns standing at her side, wiping her forehead with a cool washcloth. When Tanner wasn't holding her hand, he was
standing guard at the fetal monitor, closely watching
the scratch of the needles.

"Time to go to work," Dr. Delia finally said. "Are you
ready to push?"

It was hard work, even with the epidural, and it took
every bit of Rebecca's strength and concentration. But
she had her loving husband and mother right beside her,
offering what comfort and support they could, so she
focused and pushed for all she was worth.

After one last big push, the baby came out. Then...
total silence.

Delia handed the baby over to a nurse and praised Rebecca on a job well-done.

"He's a beautiful baby boy," Delia said.

"Yes, but—" Rebecca started, her pulse slamming into her temple. No one appeared to be panicking, but she wouldn't be able to breathe until she heard—

"Wah! Wah!" Their son protested his introduction into the big, light-filled world.

Without even so much as swaddling him, the nurse laid him in Rebecca's arms.

"He's a little more than a week early but is fully developed and in perfect shape."

Tanner was grinning like the proud daddy he was. Peggy was crying.

Rebecca just stared at her precious baby. She counted the tiniest fingers and toes she'd ever seen. Then she just gazed into her son's eyes—the same clear blue as his father's.

After a few minutes, the nurse had to take the baby to get cleaned up and weighed. Then he was swaddled and returned to Rebecca's arms.

"No," she said. "Give him to his daddy to hold."

The nurse turned to Tanner, who looked as nervous as a mouse in a room full of cats.

Rebecca smiled encouragingly. "You can do this, sweetheart. Your son wants to meet you."

"Speaking of wanting to meet the baby," Peggy said, "Jo is in the waiting room with Mackenzie."

Tanner carefully sat down on a chair, never taking his eyes off the baby.

"Well, send them in!" Rebecca insisted.

"We're just dying to see this little tyke, aren't we, Mackenzie?" Jo exclaimed as she led the little girl into the room. "I want specifics. How tall is he? How much does he weigh?"

Delia answered those questions. Eight pounds, six ounces and twenty-two inches long.

The baby gave a hearty wail and Jo laughed. "Strong lungs, too!"

Mackenzie had frozen in the middle of the room, staring at the baby and then back at Rebecca.

"Is that the baby from Auntie 'Becca's tummy?"

"He sure is," Tanner said. "Come on over here, Mackenzie, and meet your baby cousin."

The little girl went from frozen to frenzy, excitedly running over to see the baby up close.

"He's wrinkly," she said, reaching out her index finger to touch the baby's cheek. "But his skin is really soft."

"Sit down beside your uncle Tanner and he'll help you hold your cousin," Rebecca said gently, her heart warming at how excited the little girl was.

Her eyes as wide as saucers, Mackenzie sat down next to Tanner and he propped the baby in Mackenzie's arms, always keeping both hands on the baby himself.

"What do you think?"

"We get to keep him? He'll come home with us?"

Tanner's gaze met Rebecca's.

Mackenzie had called the ranch her home.

Rebecca answered her question. "Baby and I have to stay overnight and then we'll be coming home tomorrow morning. Will you make sure his crib is all ready to go?"

Mackenzie nodded solemnly.

"He's a beautiful baby," said Jo, "but I do have one question."

"What's that?" Rebecca asked.

"Does he have a name or are you just going to call him Baby Hamilton for the rest of his life? It'll do for now, but I'm expecting he probably won't like it much when he gets to be a teenager."

Tanner and Rebecca looked at each other and laughed. Tanner placed the baby in Rebecca's arms and settled next to her, leaning his hip on the side of the bed.

"We most certainly do have a name, and we think it's perfect. Everyone, meet Chase Michael Hamilton."

* * * * *

Don't miss the latest heartwarming stories about surprise babies leading to lasting love in the Cowboy Country miniseries:

The Cowboy's Surprise Baby
The Cowboy's Twins
Mistletoe Daddy
The Cowboy's Baby Blessing
And Cowboy Makes Three
A Christmas Baby for the Cowboy

Find these and other great reads at www.LoveInspired.com

Dear Reader,

This is my final story from Serendipity, and Texas's First Annual Bachelors and Baskets Auction benefiting the senior center. Tanner and Rebecca have a much different relationship than my other heroes and heroines. They're a married couple, separated by time, distance and heartbreak. But when Rebecca comes back to town with a case of amnesia, will they find their second chance?

This book was difficult for me to write. I always have humor in my books, but this one dealt with the heartbreaking subjects of infertility and stillbirth. I pray that any of my readers who've experienced infertility or stillbirth will find comfort in our Savior's arms.

I'm always delighted to hear from you, dear readers, and I love to connect socially. To get regular updates, please sign up for my newsletter at www.debkastnerbooks.com. Come join me on Facebook at www.Facebook.com/debkastnerbooks, and you can catch me on Twitter @debkastner.

Please know that I pray for each and every one of you daily.

Dare to Dream,

Deb Kastner

COMING NEXT MONTH FROM
Love Inspired®

Available September 17, 2019

THE AMISH CHRISTMAS MATCHMAKER
Indiana Amish Brides • by Vannetta Chapman
When Annie Kauffmann's father decides to join Levi Lapp in Texas to start a
new Amish community, Annie doesn't want to go. Her wedding business is in
Indiana, so leaving's out of the question. But if Annie finds Levi a wife, he might
just give up this dream of moving...

HER AMISH HOLIDAY SUITOR
Amish Country Courtships • by Carrie Lighte
A pretend courtship with Lucy Knepp's just the cover Nick Burkholder needs to
repair the cabin his brother damaged. And agreeing means Lucy can skip holiday
festivities to work on embroidery for a Christmas fund-raiser. Will a fake courtship
between this quiet Amish woman and the unpredictable bachelor turn real?

HIS UNEXPECTED RETURN
Red Dog Ranch • by Jessica Keller
For five years, Wade Jarrett's family and ex-girlfriend believed he was dead—
until he returns to the family ranch. He knew he'd have to make amends...but he
never expected he had a daughter. Can Wade convince Cassidy Danvers he's a
changed man who deserves the title of daddy and, possibly, husband?

THEIR CHRISTMAS PRAYER
by Myra Johnson
Pastor Shaun O'Grady is ready for his next missionary assignment...until he
begins working with Brooke Willoughby on the church's Christmas outreach
program. Now Shaun is not quite sure where he belongs: overseas on his
mission trip, or right here by Brooke's side.

THE HOLIDAY SECRET
Castle Falls • by Kathryn Springer
In her birth family's hometown, Ellery Marshall plans to keep her identity hidden
until she learns more about them. But that's easier said than done when single
dad Carter Bristow and his little girl begin to tug at her heart. Could she unite
two families by Christmas?

THE TWIN BARGAIN
by Lisa Carter
After her babysitter's injured, Amber Fleming's surprised when the woman's
grandson offers to help care for her twins while she attends nursing school...until
he proposes a bargain. He'll watch the girls, if she'll use her nursing skills to care
for his grandmother. But can they keep the arrangement strictly professional?

**LOOK FOR THESE AND OTHER LOVE INSPIRED BOOKS WHEREVER
BOOKS ARE SOLD, INCLUDING MOST BOOKSTORES, SUPERMARKETS,
DISCOUNT STORES AND DRUGSTORES.**

LICNM0919

SPECIAL EXCERPT FROM

Love Inspired

*Could a pretend Christmastime courtship
lead to a forever match?*

Read on for a sneak preview of
Her Amish Holiday Suitor, *part of Carrie Lighte's
Amish Country Courtships miniseries.*

Nick took his seat next to her and picked up the reins,
but before moving onward, he said, "I don't understand it,
Lucy. Why is my caring about you such an awful thing?"
His voice was quivering and Lucy felt a pang of guilt. She
knew she was overreacting. Rather, she was reacting to
a heartache that had plagued her for years, not one Nick
had caused that evening.

"I don't expect you to understand," she said, wiping
her rough woolen mitten across her cheeks.

"But I want to. Can't you explain it to me?"

Nick's voice was so forlorn Lucy let her defenses drop.
"I've always been treated like this, my entire life. *Lucy's
too weak, too fragile, too small, she can't go outside or
run around or have any fun because she'll get sick. She'll
stop breathing. She'll wind up in the hospital.* My whole
life, Nick. And then the one little taste of utter abandon I
ever experienced—charging through the dark with a frosty
wind whisking against my face, feeling totally invigorated
and alive… You want to take that away from me, too."

She was crying so hard her words were barely
intelligible, but Nick didn't interrupt or attempt to quiet
her. When she finally settled down and could speak

LIEXP0919

normally again, she sniffed and asked, "May I use your handkerchief, please?"

"Sorry, I don't have one," Nick said. "But here, you can use my scarf. I don't mind."

The offer to use Nick's scarf to dry her eyes and blow her nose was so ridiculous and sweet all at once it caused Lucy to chuckle. "*Neh*, that's okay," she said, removing her mittens to dab her eyes with her bare fingers.

"I really am sorry," he repeated.

Lucy was embarrassed. "That's all right. I've stopped blubbering. I don't need a handkerchief after all."

"*Neh*, I mean I'm sorry I treated you in a way that made you feel…the way you feel. I didn't mean to. I was concerned. I care about you and I wouldn't want anything to happen to you. I especially wouldn't want to play a role in hurting you."

Lucy was overwhelmed by his words. No man had ever said anything like that to her before, even in friendship. "It's not your fault," she said. "And I do appreciate that you care. But I'm not as fragile as you think I am."

"Fragile? You? I don't think you're fragile at all, even if you are prone to pneumonia." Nick scoffed. "I think you're one of the most resilient women I've ever known."

Lucy was overwhelmed again. If this kept up, she was going to fall hard for Nick Burkholder. Maybe she already had.

Don't miss
Her Amish Holiday Suitor *by Carrie Lighte,*
available October 2019 wherever
Love Inspired® books and ebooks are sold.

www.LoveInspired.com

Copyright © 2019 by Carrie Lighte

LIEXP0919